THE IDEAL COUPLE

Before the ball was to begin, Lord Duncan Kedrington, fresh from the talented hands of his valet, presented himself for his wife's approval. His dark blue coat was beautifully cut, his white waistcoat was impeccable, and his cravat was tied in a style that Brummel himself would have envied.

"You do look elegant," Antonia told him, "as always."

"And as always," he replied, "you, my love, look delicious."

The look that he gave Antonia promised much not only for the dazzling night ahead but for hours of delight when they were alone together after the ball had ended. Antonia could not imagine that she would ever want any man but him. It was as impossible as dear Duncan's ever wanting any other woman but her.

Or was it?

How well did Antonia know her husband?

How well did she know herself?

My
Lady Mischief

Elisabeth Kidd

A SIGNET BOOK

SIGNET
Published by the Penguin Group
Penguin Books USA Inc., 375 Hudson Street,
New York, New York 10014, U.S.A.
Penguin Books Ltd, 27 Wrights Lane,
London W8 5TZ, England
Penguin Books Australia Ltd,
Ringwood, Victoria, Australia
Penguin Books Canada Ltd, 10 Alcorn Avenue,
Toronto, Ontario, Canada M4V 3B2
Penguin Books (N.Z.) Ltd, 182–190 Wairau Road,
Auckland 10, New Zealand

Penguin Books Ltd, Registered Offices:
Harmondsworth, Middlesex, England

First published by Signet, an imprint of Dutton Signet,
a division of Penguin Books USA Inc.

First Printing, July, 1997
10 9 8 7 6 5 4 3 2 1

*This book is dedicated to
Nancy Sawyer.*

The author wishes to thank the staff of the British Museum for the information they so kindly provided about the Elgin marbles and to assure her readers that any errors of fact are hers alone and that no such incidents ever occurred as are portrayed here.

Chapter 1

❦

"Oh, dear," said Lady Kedrington with a long-suffering sigh. "Carey has got himself betrothed—again."

Her husband, who had chosen just that moment to come up behind her and begin nibbling lightly at the alabaster expanse of skin sweeping from Antonia's neck into the low décolletage of her evening gown, paid no attention to this announcement of the latest familial crisis. He and Antonia's brother had been through too many campaigns together for him to worry about Carey's surviving this one.

"Duncan!" Antonia exclaimed as his hands came around her waist and began moving gently upward. But her mind was elsewhere, and as she made no further attempt to stop him, Viscount Kedrington continued his exploration of the velvet zone beneath her cheekbone.

"Hmmm?" he murmured, deep in contemplation.

She turned slightly in his arms and waved Carey's letter at him. "He wants to marry Elena Melville."

"What? The Greek statue?"

That gave even his lordship pause. He removed one hand from his wife's waist and took the letter from her. "Did he soften her, or did she flatten him?"

"Don't be vulgar. I'm sure she is a perfectly delightful girl—underneath."

He laughed. "I am prepared to concede her hidden depths, my love, and I confess that I would be interested to hear the tale of this courtship—but you must concede that her reputation is not such to give one to hope for another Antonia Fairfax."

It was true that Elena Melville was known among the *ton* more for her cool disposition than her warm Mediterranean features—her raven hair, olive complexion, and large, melancholy dark eyes being scarcely in fashion. Her fortune had attracted numerous suitors who, at least until now, could not in the end weather her unspoken disdain. Lady Kedrington's golden hair and wide blue eyes, containing just a hint of mischief, were much more à la mode, and her warm nature much more universally appealing. But Antonia was very thoroughly married, as all her would-be cisisbeos constantly regretted.

Indeed, Kedrington thought, watching his wife put the finishing touches on her toilette, Antonia was even lovelier now than when they were married two years before—and it was not only her doting husband who said so. But he alone was aware that of late she had been subject to a restlessness that he could only attribute to the continued lack of a child to complete their happiness. There was time enough for that, he knew, although he did not attempt to convince her of it. He had learned not to raise the subject, for she would only make a joke of it—and then turn away to conceal the hurt in her eyes. Instead, he strove to fill her time with travel and amusements, and to spoil her with numerous servants and extravagant gifts until the day that the magic should, without her realizing it, happen.

Meanwhile, they continued on their social round, each of them pretending there was not even that one tiny cloud on their horizon. The Kedringtons were not only the most popular hosts, but also the most sought-after guests in London, for any hostess could count on their being charming to the most tiresome relation and enlivening any evening that threatened to languish, even if their notions of amusement were often unorthodox and occasionally even scandalous. The *ton* remembered afterward only that the event had been a success.

The occasion immediately before them was a reception in honor of Thomas Bruce, Lord Elgin—or more precisely, in honor of his lordship's infamous collection of antiquities emancipated from the Acropolis in Athens when Elgin was posted there as ambassador to the Ottoman Porte.

The Act of Parliament transferring ownership of the so-called Elgin marbles to the nation had been passed only the week before, so the Drummonds were well to the front of the pack in making use of them as the excuse for yet another *ton* party. Sir John had been a member of Parliament for twenty years, long enough to insinuate himself into the inner circles of both houses of that institution and thus be privy to even the most incidental news before it became public—hence the invitation that arrived at the Kedringtons' Brook Street house on the very morning that the *Times* announced passage of the bill.

"Will Lord Elgin actually put in an appearance?" Lady Kedrington asked her husband an hour later, as they waited in their carriage in the parade of vehicles disgorging guests at the entrance to the Drummond mansion on Cavendish Square. "I was under the impression that there is no political love lost between Lord Elgin and Sir John."

"Sir John is that singular combination—a shrewd politician and an astute patron of the arts. Even had he disagreed with Elgin's behavior as ambassador, he would have voted for the purchase of the marbles only to keep them in the country. In any case, he would not be so rash as to let politics intrude on a social occasion—particularly one that will win him praise for being a good fellow."

"Which means," Antonia concluded, "that Lord Elgin *will* attend so as not to be seen to be any less gracious to the honorable opposition."

"Well put, my love. You are beginning to understand politics after all."

"Enough to know that I am glad you never went in for it."

"Do you think I should have?"

"I don't think you *could* have. You may be secretive, but you are not devious."

"Thank you. I think."

"It *was* meant as a compliment."

"Very well, and you may accept my compliments on your political astuteness."

"But . . . ?" Antonia prodded, knowing there was more to come.

His lordship smiled and began ticking buts off on his fingers. "First, Elgin no longer sits in the Lords. Second, he has recently endured lengthy and sordid divorce proceedings, which have done nothing to alleviate the dire financial situation he contracted in the service of his nation. Third, and finally, he suffers from a physical disfigurement—likewise contracted in his country's service— which precludes his even walking about in public without being recognized. In short, he *won't* come."

Antonia, suspecting another reason behind this catalogue of Elgin's trials, glared at her husband. "Do not attempt to play on my sympathy for his lordship's misfortunes, Duncan, believing it will change my mind about the marbles. I am sorry for him, but as ambassador, I consider him to have been acting in his nation's behalf, which makes the rest of us as liable for his actions as he is—and I resent being made a party to the affair."

The national debate over the marbles had settled into the Kedrington household as a permanent topic of conversation, but when her ladyship touched on that particular theme, the viscount generally considered it politic to end the discussion. He now lapsed into silence, and after several moments remarked only, "Did Carey say when he would deign to call and introduce the Greek statue to his family?"

"Momentarily, according to his letter—although as usual he was annoyingly unspecific. And you *are* being evasive."

"Better than devious."

Antonia laid her head back on the squabs and plied her

fan languidly. "June is too sultry for subtleties," she observed with a sigh. "I expect we are in for another spell of wet weather. Where do you suppose Carey could have met Miss Melville?"

"Perhaps he's reformed his behavior and been allowed back into polite society and near places of public accommodation," Kedrington remarked. "We can go to Brighton if you like."

"No, I think not," Antonia said vaguely, referring, he assumed, to Brighton. Their private conversation tended to be laced with non sequiturs and obscure references that generally made perfect sense to both of them, but when one's mind wandered, the point tended to do so as well.

Kedrington feared that he sometimes guessed wrongly about what Antonia was thinking, although she had never given him any indication that he was not living up to her fondest expectations of the married state. He wished he could make her perfectly happy, but knew that after two years, he was still feeling his way very cautiously toward that goal.

A moment later, they were let down at the Drummonds' front door, and Antonia came back to life. She always enjoyed parties, and although Sir John and Lady Drummond were not what she would ever consider intimate friends, they had a spacious, elegant house and did not pinch pennies where food and drink were concerned.

"Oh, dear," she said when they had been announced and she surveyed the crowded room with delighted anticipation. "Where do we begin?"

Kedrington followed her glance, nodding his head at several acquaintances, but resisting tacit invitations to join their various circles. From his superior height, he spotted a waiter bearing a tray of champagne glasses and steered Antonia in that direction. Deftly lifting four glasses off the tray with his two hands as they passed the bemused waiter, he offered two to her.

"This should smooth our passage into society."

In unison, they drank one glass of wine each, then sought out their hosts.

Lady Drummond was a tall, handsome woman with impeccable social address, but not an ounce of humor in her makeup. For this reason, Antonia admired her, but did not like her, as she was herself unable to maintain a conversation for more than a few minutes without making a joke. And while she did not require that people laugh at her jokes, she did expect them to understand that what she had said was in fact meant in jest.

Lady Drummond had, however, mastered the exercise of moving her lips into a smile, and she performed this maneuver smoothly when Antonia greeted her and thanked her prettily for the honor of her invitation. Lady Drummond remarked no irony in this speech, and her smile warmed notably when she extended her hand to Kedrington.

"My lord, I am pleased to see you," she said, almost flirtatiously.

Disregarding his wife's quizzical glance, Kedrington bowed over the gloved hand extended to him and raised it fleetingly to his lips. "The pleasure is ours, Lady Drummond. You have a goodly crowd, I see."

Sir John laughed at that and said, "You need not say that as if this were intended to be a political rally, Kedrington. I assure you, our only motives this evening are to celebrate the glories of our new national treasure."

"Why, how stupid of me," Antonia said guilelessly. "I thought they were *Greek* national treasures."

"You must forgive my wife, Sir John," Kedrington said. "She is firmly planted in the anti-Elgin faction—which may perhaps be the first time she finds herself on the same side of any argument as Lord Byron."

"Ah, yes," offered Lady Drummond. " 'The Curse of Minerva.' Such a melodramatic poem . . . and so much scenery to endure before one finds the explanation of the title. It is full of allegory, of course."

"Like the banks of the Nile," Kedrington murmured so that only Antonia could hear, but she pretended not to.

"I am *not* in the Byron faction," she said, making her stand on political rather than literary grounds. "I am perfectly aware that had Lord Elgin not removed the marbles from the Parthenon, the French would likely have done so had the Turks not carried them off first to pound into plaster. Nevertheless, we ought to have tried harder to persuade the Greeks to protect their own statues—or bribed them to do so, since Lord Elgin did not scruple to display his blunt."

This snippet of vulgar cant caused Lady Drummond to raise her brows, but as Antonia went blithely on voicing her opinion that the marbles ought never to have been moved from their natural setting, her hostess's silent admonition went unheeded.

"There was nothing natural about it," Lady Kedrington's husband pointed out. "They were man-made objects in a man-made edifice, not trees in a forest."

"You will forgive my mentioning it, Lady Kedrington," said Sir John, vastly amused by her passion, "but the Greeks had very little to say to the matter. And their Turkish rulers appear to have little regard for art."

"May we hope that Lord Elgin will put in an appearance tonight?" Kedrington asked, steering the conversation into waters that, if not calmer, might at least prove less deep.

"He sent his regrets," Lady Drummond said, a little tartly, as if miffed that her invitation did not bring the savior of Greece—or the plunderer of the Parthenon, according to one's lights—running to show his gratitude for her patronage. "Lord Aberdeen, one of his staunchest allies, is here, *and*," her ladyship finished triumphantly, "Sir Thomas Lawrence will join us for a cold supper later. Indeed, if you will forgive me for a moment, I shall go and see that the punch is well iced."

With that, Lady Drummond sailed majestically away, remarking in her wake that the Kedringtons must not fail to view the marbles in the upstairs salon.

"Good heavens," Antonia exclaimed. "Surely, you do not have any of the actual pieces here?"

"Certainly not in the upstairs salon," said Sir John. "We should scarcely have been able to drag one of them into the hall without widening the door. No, what we have are some very fine drawings that I commissioned from a young artist friend of mine. He took them from the original pieces while they were still in Elgin's house in Park Lane. Mr. Metaxis is a talented young man, if somewhat over-heated on occasion. Only to be expected of a Greek, I daresay, in the presence of his . . . er, patrimony."

"I should like to see his drawings," Antonia said, glancing at her husband to see if he would accompany her, but his eyes were directed elsewhere.

"Lady Sefton has just come in," he observed. "Did you not say you hoped to speak with her tonight?"

"Oh, yes," Antonia said, diverted, then smiled at her host. "Do forgive me, Sir John, but I must conduct some necessary female business tonight before giving myself up to Greek drawings and iced punch."

Sir John bowed and then gazed admiringly at her as she glided gracefully away and murmured, "Lovely."

"I like her."

Sir John laughed. "You're a lucky dog, Kedrington. Don't blame the rest of us for admiring from afar what we cannot hope to approach. What does she want from Maria Sefton, by the way?"

"An entrée to Almack's for one of her protégées, of course."

"I might have guessed. Never could see why that place is such a magnet, myself. It's crowded, hot, and the refreshments are insipid at best."

"One could say the same about White's."

Sir John chuckled and concurred. "One conducts one's business where one must, I suppose."

"Why *are* you supporting Elgin this way, Drummond?" Kedrington asked, but did not succeed in catching Sir John far enough off his guard to surprise a direct answer out of him.

"I was on the select committee that recommended the purchase of the collection, you know."

"Why?"

Drummond smiled. "Always the skeptic, eh, Kedrington? Can you impute no noble motives to me?"

"Not to any politician."

"Ah. Yes, you've always had that blind spot. Very well. If not noble, I can at least be candid. I did it because I believe the marbles *will* in the end be accepted as a national treasure—a *British* national treasure—and I shall not hesitate to take as much of the credit as I can. There are more important matters coming up in the next Parliament, and a reputation for being forward-looking never hurt anyone— certainly no Tory. It is only the Whigs who seem able to make insight look like radicalism."

Kedrington laughed. "You are an opportunist, John, pure and simple."

"Of course," Drummond agreed, unapologetically. "And thirty-five thousand pounds is a small price to pay for a golden opportunity, particularly since it did not come out of my own purse. I do not doubt the artistic value of the collection, so my approval of Elgin's ambassadorial conduct was a mere gesture."

"It was a particularly small price to pay compared to Elgin's outlay—I understand that it cost him twice as much to collect and ship the marbles in the first place."

"He should be grateful that they were not packed back to Greece at once, a victim of the economic zeal of the current administration—which behaves like a housewife who suddenly finds she cannot afford a pint of beer, and so economizes by not buying bread."

"Have you no loyalties, John?"

Drummond smiled. "Certainly. But as long as no one knows what they are, and my favor continues to be courted in the hope of gaining my vote, I shall continue to enjoy a successful parliamentary career. In pursuit of which, my dear Kedrington, I shall now go and flatter Aberdeen, who I see has been left temporarily without sycophants."

"Beware climbing too high too quickly," Kedrington advised. "The way down can be precipitous."

"I shall keep a good foothold," Drummond assured him with a parting smile.

It was some time before Kedrington was once again able to speak with his wife, both having numerous acquaintances, singly or in common, with whom they felt obliged to spend at least a few minutes in conversation. It was not until Kedrington noticed that Antonia's bon mots were beginning to be conveyed to him secondhand by some of their mutual acquaintances that he pointedly steered himself back in her direction.

"What a devious man," she remarked when he cornered her near a niche containing a statue of Apollo.

"Who?"

"Sir John, of course. I suspect he has his eye on a peerage one day—why else does he insinuate himself so cozily with Aberdeen, and I daresay every other member of the Upper House? And have you never noticed the way he assesses whomever he is speaking with for their reactions to his words before he has scarcely uttered them? I am certain he has hidden motives beneath his ulterior reasons."

She held out her empty goblet to him. "I should like another glass of champagne."

"You should have some supper as well, or you'll get tipsy," Kedrington said, taking the glass from her and setting it down on Apollo's plinth.

"If I eat any more of those lobster patties, I'll get fat and you'll divorce me."

"It would be cheaper to keep you in lobster patties."

"Beast."

"I think you underestimate Sir John," Kedrington said, contemplating Apollo.

"Yes, I daresay he is more devious than even I give him credit for."

"Possibly, but not necessarily to a dishonorable end. Observe this statue, for example."

She did so. "A copy of the Apollo Belvedere?"

"Indeed. It used to stand in the small rotunda as you enter the house."

"I remember. Why has he hidden it away back here?"

"He told me he approved Elgin's actions because he believes the marbles have artistic merit. Yet the Parthenon figures are so far from the aesthetic ideal that Apollo here represents, they force one to look at art with new eyes. Politicians such as Sir John are notoriously incapable of looking at *anything* in a new way. He therefore risks appearing a dilettante to his peers in order to enlighten them—a risky course."

Lady Kedrington greeted this speech with a resentful look. "I wish, Duncan, that you were not so clever at making me see six sides to a two-sided issue. Now you have made an honest man of Sir John, and I suppose I shall be obliged to invite him to our little soirée next week."

"Which little soirée is that?"

"The one in honor of Carey's betrothal."

"I'm glad to hear that we have reduced the celebration from a ball to a mere soirée, considering Carey's past poor finishes in the matrimonial stakes—not to mention that we have yet to actually see him and Miss Melville in the same place at the same time. Although Lady Drummond informs me that Carey accepted her invitation to this affair, that may have been before he was distracted by Miss Melville's acceptance of his proposal. I daresay they will not put in an appearance here after all."

"The evening is young. I daresay we can amuse ourselves while we wait and see."

Kedrington leaned closer to whisper into her ear, "I'd rather wait at home."

She slapped his hand, which had wandered onto a private preserve, with her fan. He sighed exaggeratedly and picked up her empty glass.

"Would you rather have your champagne glass refilled,

my arm to lead you to the supper room, or a look at the drawings upstairs?"

"I should like some supper—*and* more champagne, and *then* a look at the drawings."

"Greedy woman."

"Whose fault is that?"

He had no answer.

Chapter 2

❦

"Dash it all, Elena," exclaimed Mr. Fairfax. "Why can't I kiss you? We're going to be married, aren't we?"

"Of course you may kiss me," Miss Melville replied calmly. Elena was always calm. "But not in quite so public a place, if you please. What will people think?"

"They will think I'm besotted with you," Carey murmured against Elena's earlobe, "and they will be right."

Miss Melville permitted Mr. Fairfax's lips to brush hers in an exploratory gesture, but when his hand came up to move her chin more in his direction, she brushed it away and exclaimed, not entirely without regret, "Carey! Do behave yourself! What if someone saw us?"

"A hackney coach is as private as we ever seem to get," Carey grumbled, sitting back on his side of the vehicle with an exaggerated sigh.

It had been the devil of a to-do to persuade Elena's guardian to consent to her driving alone with Carey even the short distance to the Drummond reception, although Carey suspected that Arthur Melville's mixed feelings about their destination preoccupied him more than his ward's reputation. Melville had social-climbing ambitions for Elena, and while privately he expressed admiration for Lord Elgin's actions in acquiring the Parthenon marbles, he had told Carey frankly that he was reluctant to expose Elena to a situation that might result in half of London society condemning her for the company she kept.

Mr. Fairfax found this mildly insulting, as if his engagement to Miss Melville did not provide her with sufficient protection from censure on either side, but not wishing to exacerbate the already delicate relationship between himself and Elena's guardian, he had only pointed out that his sister and brother-in-law—who were themselves on opposite sides of the controversy although in perfect harmony otherwise—would be at the reception. The mention of Viscount Kedrington reanimated Melville's social awareness enough that, in the end, he permitted Mr. Fairfax to escort his ward to the reception.

Carey had not revealed to Melville that he intended to surprise his sister by appearing with Elena at the Drummonds' and had therefore not informed either her or Kedrington that he would come. It had seemed an excellent notion to demonstrate from the outset how well his future bride would pass muster amongst the sorts of persons whose company Carey personally found tiresome but whose approval he was well aware his wife should have. This strategy would also spare Elena the prolonged anticipation of a prearranged meeting to be interviewed, however cordially, for her future position. His brother-in-law, he well knew, could be formidable until one got on his good side.

Apart from all these considerations, he could not, until the last minute, be assured of gaining Melville's approval for the evening's program. But gazing at his intended in the dim light of the conveyance now rattling along Wigmore Street, he reflected that, had Melville proved obdurate after all, and even if Kedrington gave her one of his snubs, he would have fought very hard to have Elena beside him as she was now. He had never met anyone quite like Elena, and the more he was with her, the more fascinating she became.

It was not that he had not looked long and hard for a suitable bride. His sister had despaired of his ever making up his mind to marry, and his brother-in-law made sly jokes about his trying on new girls like new hats—a different one for every occasion and every season. Carey had said he did not know what he was looking for, but he would know it when he saw it and he could not overlook any possibility. However, when he found what he sought, it was not what he had expected. And he had not expected to find it in Elena Melville.

He had in fact seen Elena two or three times at the kind of large gathering where Carey had been wont to wear his latest feminine decoration on his arm, before he came to understand that while some young ladies' brilliance was ephemeral, the gold beneath Elena's earthenware exterior was the genuine article.

Kedrington had accused him of giving the various candidates for his hand a trial run at filling the social niche his fortune and connections would give her—and the results were, admittedly, variable. One shy thing had declared breathlessly afterward that one ridotto was quite enough for her, thank you, and that was the last he saw of her. Another, more ambitious girl found that she quite liked having the power to cut other people, but thought she could find a more powerful consort to support her in this aspiration.

Now that Carey came to remember it, on the third occasion that he had encountered Elena Melville, they did not speak, as he was escorting yet another matrimonial candidate at the time. Elena made an obviously acute assessment of the situation, and when her horse passed his on Rotten Row, she gave him a withering look that spoke eloquently of her opinion of him as a fribble, good for nothing but being decorative at parties or making a fourth for whist. That had irked him—in no small part because he suspected that she was right and that he was turning into just such a charming but useless hanger-on.

The next time he saw her, fortunately, she seemed not even to remember him. At first he thought it was because he did not have a girl hanging on his arm—the latest having declined his offer of marriage coolly but not entirely heartlessly, assuring him that he was a dependable friend and expressing the hope that he would find some lady who found dependability romantic enough to marry for.

On the occasion—Carey remembered afterward that it was a Tuesday and there had been a brisk March breeze—he had been walking down Baker Street early in the morning following one of the rare evenings nowadays that he spent among exclusively male companions, one of whom had put him up for the night, when the sound of children squabbling in a small private square to his right caught his ear. He would have passed by, but a different voice, feminine yet authoritative, rose above the hubbub.

Carey rose on his toes to peer over the bush just inside the garden fence and saw Elena Melville holding a freckled youngster firmly by the ear and lecturing him on the injustice of picking on someone smaller than he—his victim being, apparently, the curly-haired little girl sitting on a bench and sobbing.

"You see?" Elena said, giving the ear a sharp tug. "It's not such sport when someone bigger turns on *you*, is it?"

"She took our ball!" protested another girl, whom Carey judged by her freckles to be the miscreant's older sister, in a whining tone.

"No, you kicked it at her, and she quite naturally picked it up," Elena said, adding firmly, "I saw her."

The freckled girl poked her bottom lip out belligerently, but said no more, and Elena pressed her case. "I'm sure that the young lady would have returned the ball to you in another moment if you had only given her the chance before attacking her."

"I never—" persisted the boy, but Elena cut him off.

"And it would have been gentlemanly of you to ask her to join your game, don't you think? As for you, miss"—Elena turned on the older girl, who was now smirking in a superior way at her brother—"you must learn to have a little more sympathy to others of your sex. You never know when you will need their goodwill."

When no further defense was forthcoming, Elena shooed the older children away and sat on the bench for a few minutes with the smaller girl. Carey could not hear what was said, but five minutes later, the child skipped happily away, apparently none the worse for her unfortunate encounter. He applauded lightly.

Elena, startled, looked up. A frown sketched her forehead but—much to Carey's astonishment—disappeared when she recognized him.

"Good morning, Mr. Fairfax."

Carey tipped his hat and contrived not to trip over his tongue. "Good morning, Miss Melville. That was a salutary lesson you delivered."

She sighed. "I fear it will make no difference. The Allenbury children receive no discipline at home and nothing an outsider may say will make any difference."

"Still, you made the effort. And you seem to have a way with children."

An expression that seemed to Carey very like sadness crossed Elena's face briefly, but it was gone before he could be sure. She rose briskly from the bench and approached the garden gate, which Carey quickly opened for her. She paused, studying him—as if, he thought, he were something on display in a vegetable barrow—and said, "Would you be kind enough to walk me home, Mr. Fairfax?"

"My pleasure, Miss Melville," he said, seizing the opportunity to offer his arm. He valiantly essayed no further conversation—fearing to say the wrong thing and remind her of what a fribble he was—until she ventured to inquire politely about his health. He responded suitably to this opening, and after an unexceptional ten-minute stroll, he delivered her to her doorstep in good order; she smiled when she bade him good-day, and Carey felt he had won a victory.

Following this incident, Carey began to hope that Miss Melville's opinion of him had taken a turn upward, and he made strenuous efforts to improve it still further. He was not quite sure why he did this, except that their brief conversation by the garden gate had given him much food for thought. He was not at all certain of what lay behind Elena's remarks or her sudden desire for his company.

Indeed, when she agreed to pay a visit—accompanied by her guardian, of course—to Carey's country home in Leicester, he was both elated and wary. He had heard more than enough tales from his army cronies about scheming females who knew to a nicety how to bring a fellow up to scratch only for the pleasure of turning the poor clunch down when he came to make an offer.

On the third hand—Carey often found himself weighing the myriad possible outcomes to their strange courtship in this way—Elena was scarcely your typical female. She was unencumbered by an avaricious mama; indeed, Mr. Melville encouraged Carey's suit with an ill grace. Elena's fortune was not large, but neither was it so small that she needed to marry money. She appeared to have no interest in cutting a dash in society—indeed, she shuddered at the very idea. Perhaps she wanted only to settle down and raise a family. But any reasonably presentable fellow would do for that. Why did she choose him?

"Dash it, Elena," he said finally, exasperated. "Why don't you marry me and put me out of my misery?"

As soon as the words were out of his mouth, he realized that this was the most unromantic proposal he had ever made, although certainly the most heartfelt.

They were riding in the springtime glory of England's finest hunting country at the time, and Carey reined in and reached for the reins of Elena's mare to bring her around to face him.

"I'm sorry—"

She put a gloved hand lightly over his mouth to stop him. "For what? For proposing to me so impulsively? Did you not mean to do so when I accepted your invitation to come to Wyckham?"

"Is that what . . . I mean, I did, yes, but I never . . ."

She smiled. It was not something she did often, but it lighted her face like the sun and made him feel she did it for him alone and no other. It was then that he stopped wondering and knew he was in love with her.

"I will marry you, Carey," she said simply.

For the next few days, he walked on air, nodding happily whenever Elena made some suggestion about their wedding, which was to be in the summer—much too long a wait for Carey's taste and a shockingly short time in Elena's opinion, but it was the compromise they finally reached. He came down to earth only long enough to write to his sister that he had found the perfect bride. Elena was the most beautiful, mysterious, and fascinating woman he had ever met. He could scarcely wait to introduce her to his family and watch them be fascinated too.

To this end, therefore, Carey had contrived his scheme to bring Elena to the Drummonds' reception, and by the time he handed her down from the hackney in front of the Cavendish Square mansion, he was fixed in his determination to show her off to all and sundry as his future bride.

Somewhat to his disappointment, their entrance at the reception caused nary a ripple in the social current. Elena, however, confessed that she was relieved to find they were not the center of all eyes—or of any eyes, so far as Carey could tell—and she became a little braver.

Carey scowled. "I don't see Kedrington or my sister anywhere. I hope we haven't missed them."

"Do you see our hostess? We ought to greet her before anything. Perhaps she can tell us if the Kedringtons have left."

Lady Drummond was her gracious self, although Carey did not fail to notice the curious inspection she bestowed on Elena—rather as if she could not decide whether Miss Melville's presence on this occasion was a social coup or a come-down.

"You were kind to invite me, ma'am," Elena said warmly, as if she had been welcomed with open arms. Carey admired her poise more than ever. He had always thought Lady Drummond an old battle-ax, but she actually smiled on him—at least he thought it was a smile—as if bestowing her approval on them both.

"Almost as good as a voucher for Almack's, by Jove!" Carey muttered as they made their excuses and went in search of Antonia, whom Lady Drummond advised them would very likely be found in the upstairs salon.

"What can you mean?" Elena asked.

"Sorry, love, I was just being a clunch again. Of course, you wouldn't know what I meant. I say, there's Cedric Maitland. Haven't seen him in an age."

Elena stopped him before he could dash off to greet an old friend. "Please, Carey, let us find your sister first. If I do not meet her soon, I shall die of anticipation. I'm so afraid she won't like me."

"Stuff and nonsense. Antonia likes everyone—I mean, she really likes the people she likes, and she makes up her mind in an instant when she decides to dislike someone."

Elena looked stricken.

"Dash it, I'm putting that all wrong again. Look, let's go find her first thing, shall we? I haven't seen Duncan—my brother-in-law, Kedrington, you know—for an age."

As it happened, Lady Kedrington was looking out from the alcove in which the marble Apollo—and her very much livelier husband—were entertaining her, and saw her brother and his betrothed enter before they saw her, which gave her an opportunity, when she had recovered from her surprise, to scrutinize Miss Melville.

She had seen her before only at a distance and had never been introduced, but her initial impression of a quiet, almost drab girl proved on closer inspection to be unjust. True, Elena was not a fashionable beauty, but her features were regular, almost classical, with a straight nose, full lips, and large dark eyes. Her heavy, almost black hair was parted in the middle and drawn back into an elaborate knot, lacking the usual flirtatious tendrils hanging from it. Her gown was plain but of good quality and a flattering shade of dark green, and she wore only a cameo broach on a green ribbon and a pair of simple earbobs in the way of ornamentation. Everything about her, indeed, was plain but of high quality. Antonia hoped that her character would prove of a similar high order.

She nudged Kedrington, then smiled and waved at Carey to catch his attention. She hurried forward to greet him.

"Dearest, most *distressing* brother of mine, here you are back in town so soon! I vow, your letter arrived only today and sent me into quite a tizzy. But at least my curiosity to meet Miss Melville is quickly satisfied, and for that I suppose I must be grateful to you."

She held out a hand, which Elena took with a tentative smile. "Pay no attention to my chatter, my dear, it is only to cover my nervousness at meeting someone who will be playing such a large part in my family in future. Normally, I am quite a sensible woman, as you will learn."

"When will she learn that?" Kedrington asked, coming up just then. "I've yet to see any sign of it myself. How do you do, Miss Melville."

"Very well, thank you, my lord," Elena said.

"Good God, don't call me that or I shall feel twenty years older. Duncan—or Kedrington, if you must have a title—will do nicely among ourselves."

Carey cast his brother-in-law a look of gratitude that caused Kedrington's eyes to crinkle in amusement, but he did not embarrass Mr. Fairfax by any further acknowledgment of his brother-in-law's apprehension on subjecting Miss Melville to his mercy.

"We were just going upstairs to look at Lord Drummond's collection of drawings of the Elgin marbles, as everyone now seems to refer to them," Antonia said. "Won't you both join us?"

"Only if it's a small collection, and I can get something to eat afterward," Carey said.

Antonia took Elena's arm and patted it, and they ascended the carved marble staircase to the upper level of the mansion. "I daresay you have learned by now that Carey spends a great deal of thought on where his next meal will come from. My husband tells me that it is a habit resulting from constant privation in Spain. However, he seems to have got over it, while Carey, despite being back in this country for more than two years, has scarcely stopped eating to draw breath. Has he given you a colorful account of his adventures in Spain? I assure you, you need not believe a word of it."

Antonia went on in this voluble fashion until she felt the muscles in Elena's arm relax a little; then, when she also saw the tiny lines in her forehead disappear, she allowed Elena a few words in edgewise, and thus it was not long before they were on easy terms. Elena was not, thank goodness, one of those misses who had nothing to say for themselves; she had opinions, which she did not hesitate to voice, although only in the most discreet way, and she actually smiled at Antonia's jokes. Lady Kedrington was fast coming to like Miss Melville, and it was not until some time later that she wondered if Miss Melville had liked her in return or was merely being polite.

They had entered the salon in which the drawings were displayed, followed by the gentlemen, to whom Antonia was about to address some remark, when she felt Elena stiffen again. She glanced at her, only to find her staring fixedly ahead of her; her face had gone pale, except for two spots of bright color in her cheeks.

"My, dear, whatever is the matter?" Antonia asked, following Elena's gaze to a drawing—of a frieze of rather ferocious-looking figures that otherwise did not appear to contain anything to give even an innocent girl a fright.

Elena started, recovered herself, and stammered, "I . . . I beg your pardon. I only . . . that is, I felt faint for a moment, but it has passed already. I did not mean to startle you."

Carey heard this and hastened to offer his support, making concerned noises until Elena whispered with unusual ferocity, "Please do stop, Carey! I am perfectly well. I do not wish to go home. Let us look at the pictures now and say no more about it!"

Kedrington had fallen back to join his wife and whispered, as the young couple wandered off, "What can that have meant?"

"I'm certain it was something about this drawing," Antonia said, staring at the charcoal sketch. "But I see nothing unusual about it, do you?"

Kedrington gave it a considered study. "It is neither unusually bad nor unusually good, although it succeeds in representing its subject with reasonable objectivity. As I recall, the figures depicted are not nearly so heroic as one might suppose from this illustration, but undue license cannot be said to have been taken."

"When you go on in that erudite fashion, I know your mind is working on some other problem—what is it?"

"The same problem—Miss Melville's odd reaction to seeing this perfectly ordinary picture. However, I fear the answer will be revealed only with time, if then, so I expect we had best put it out of our minds for now."

She gazed at him, frowning slightly, but he only kissed her cheek and said, "Shall we join the youngsters again?"

Chapter 3

~

The morning following the Drummonds' reception seemed designed to improve the already excellent reputation of English springs, and Lady Kedrington, glancing out of her window, smiled back at the sun as at a good omen.

Antonia was not in general an early riser, having been, as she was the first to admit, corrupted by town ways. When she had lived in the country and run her brother's estate for him during the years while he served with the army in the Peninsula, she had been perfectly content to be up with the chickens, but two seasons in London had been sufficient to reveal to her an unexpected inclination to lie abed until at least nine, or later after an evening social event.

Thus it was unusual for her to be awake and prepared to venture into the world at ten o'clock, but she was dressed in an appropriately seasonal India muslin day dress and a villager hat with pink plumes that bounced jauntily when she moved. She had put her husband's oddly inscrutable behavior at last night's reception out of her mind even before they returned home, for her thoughts were already on how best to show Miss Melville that she would be welcomed wholeheartedly into the family.

She had begun planning a busy social schedule to introduce Elena to the rest of their circle as well, until it occurred to her that the younger lady's tastes might not run to the kind of merry, highly voluble dinners and card parties that Antonia favored. She therefore turned, as she often did when she found herself in a social quandary, to her husband's aunts, and that morning following the Drummond reception found her on her way to consult them.

Mrs. Julia Wilmot and Miss Hester Coverley resided together in a small house on Berkeley Square, the door to which was opened by their aged butler, who betrayed only by a slight slackening of the wrinkles around his rheumy eyes that he was pleased to see Lady Kedrington.

"Good morning, Webster," said her ladyship, breezing past him into the hall. "Are the ladies at home?"

This was a rhetorical question, as Mrs. Wilmot never left her house other than on two journeys a year to and from her home in Berkshire. Miss Coverley never left it before noon, although after that hour, she might be found anywhere in the city, for her acquaintance was as widespread as it was varied. Nonetheless, visitors were received only on Sundays, with the exception of family members, whose attendance was desired much more frequently, every day being the goal of the aunts, if the bane of the male members of the family. Antonia did her best to keep her husband in his aunts' good graces by anticipating every summons and forestalling them by regular visits, however brief.

"Mrs. Wilmot is in the drawing room," Webster informed her, whereupon Antonia said she would announce herself and left him standing in the hall as she opened the first door to her left. She found Julia Wilmot sitting in a chintz-covered chair, a teacup in one hand and her half-glasses on her nose, reading the *Morning Post* by the sunlight coming in the window that looked out onto the square.

Julia always looked elegant, in a way that Antonia hoped she might grow into at that age. Today, she was dressed in her customary gray, but it was a light shade, trimmed with narrow blue ribbons at the hem and sleeves, and she wore over her shoulders a fringed gray shawl that gave her an almost dashing appearance. Her complexion, nearly unlined, was that of a woman thirty years her junior, and her eyes were clear and sharp with interest in the world. Antonia knew that rheumatism kept Julia from going about in society as much as choice did, but to see her sitting gracefully in her own parlor, eager to receive visitors, one would not know she labored under any restrictions.

"Good morning, dear," Julia said, lifting her cheek to be kissed. "Have a cup of tea with me. Were you at the Drummonds' reception last night?"

"Good heavens! Never tell me it was written up in the *Post*," Antonia exclaimed, seating herself and picking up the teapot and one of the extra cups Julia kept at hand for the convenience of family visitors.

"Certainly not, foolish child. Hester told me that you and Duncan had been invited. Was Elgin there?"

"No, but a great many other people were, and I shall tell you all about it presently. But I have more important news—Carey is engaged to be married!"

"Tosh. That is not news. Who is it this time?"

Secretly pleased to be beforehand with this wonderful story, for Julia always seemed to know everything that went on in town before anyone else did, despite her self-imposed seclusion, Antonia delayed the tantalizing particulars as long as possible.

"This time I believe he has found precisely the right girl. She is neither insipid nor stupid—although not so clever that she feels obliged to flaunt her learning—and while yet young, she is not your typical beauty."

"Good gracious, not that horsey Manderville girl?"

"No, Aunt Julia, how can you insult Carey's tastes so? He never looked at Sybil Manderville."

"She has enough money to make her a diamond of the first water in some eyes. Does this new girl possess any fortune at all? What's her name?"

"I believe she is in possession of a modest fortune, but Carey need not look for an heiress. He is not extravagant."

"Perhaps not—although one would not guess it from that coat he had on when he called here last. And that estate of yours is not yet reaping sufficient profit to keep him in waistcoats, much less coats by Weston. Why isn't he home tending to his tenants, by the by?"

Antonia could see that Julia had changed her tack. Knowing that criticism of her brother, however mild, never failed to raise Antonia's defensive bristles, she would keep it up if Antonia continued to be coy about the name of Carey's intended bride. She decided to waste no more time in roundaboutation.

"She is Elena Melville."

This gave even Julia pause, although Antonia did not suppose that the brief silence that greeted her announcement betokened that Julia did not recognize the name.

"Well," she said after a moment, "this is unexpected."

Antonia smiled. "So you see why I say that this time is different. I do believe Carey sincerely loves her, and I should not be surprised if she turned out to be precisely the right wife for him, despite the . . . er, unusual appearance of the match."

"You've met her, then?"

"Yes, last night at the reception. To be sure, we spoke only very briefly. That is why I have come to you, *dearest* Aunt."

"Do not cut a wheedle with me," Julia advised forthrightly. "You know I will give you my advice whether you ask for it or not, and slicing me up sweet will not make it any more palatable if it is not the advice you seek."

Antonia smiled, more at Julia's twisting of the slang she heard secondhand from Hester than at her scarely concealed curiosity about Miss Melville.

"I would not dream of . . . er, doing such a thing," Antonia protested. "I only hoped for a suggestion from you as to how I might begin to entertain Elena, to make her feel welcome. I have the liveliest dread that my usual style of party would not be to her liking at all."

"Has the engagement been formally announced?" Julia asked.

"No, and that is another matter I wished to consult you

about. Shall we put an announcement in the *Times* at once?"

"I suppose Carey would happily shout it from the rooftops," Julia remarked, somewhat mollified by the assurance that her self-sufficient niece-by-marriage did occasionally need her advice in social matters.

Antonia smiled. "I have no doubt he would, but I believe he will defer to your advice in this matter. I suspect he is still a little unsure of his good fortune and even wary of causing Elena to think badly of him."

"It appears that your scapegrace brother is coming to his senses at last. Perhaps this Miss Melville will be a good influence on him. I should advise making friends with her first, even if you feel you have done so already. Not everyone is so readily intimate with others as you are, Antonia."

"Yes, Aunt Julia," Antonia said meekly.

"Then you may bring her to see me," Julia went on. "Say, for nuncheon on Friday. That will give me a few days to see what more I can learn about her family—discreetly, of course."

"She is of Greek extraction, an orphan, and the ward of Mr. Arthur Melville."

"We do not know him, I believe," Julia said, and Antonia wondered if the plural included Miss Coverley—which seemed unlikely, given Hester's wide-ranging acquaintance—or, even inadvertently, indicated a royal superiority. Antonia did not doubt that Julia could not only look at a king but stare him down.

"You may in the meanwhile invite her to Brook Street for dinner," Julia went on. "Just you and Duncan and Carey, and perhaps one or two amiable friends. She cannot be so timid as to find that prospect daunting."

"Oh, I do not believe she is timid," Antonia ventured. "Only . . . reserved. She certainly did not seem overwhelmed by the Drummonds."

"That is a promising sign," Julia conceded thoughtfully. "Perhaps—"

But whatever she might have said next was forestalled

by the entrance into the room of Miss Hester Coverley, the second occupant of the house, Lord Kedrington's aunt on his mother's side and a lady who could not have been more different from Julia Wilmot had they been born on different continents instead of merely in different counties.

Hester had been one of the celebrated Coverley girls in her youth, the other being Lord Kedrington's mother, Cecily, and despite her gray ringlets and plump figure, she still retained some of the beauty and all of the vivacity of her youth. As usual, she was dressed in a youthful style and carried a silk pelisse over her arm, obviously in preparation to go out. Antonia suspected that a matching bonnet awaited her in the hall, but Julia disapproved of Hester's frivolous taste in headgear, so Hester did not inflict it upon her if she could avoid it.

Hester put her head in the door and trilled, "I'm off now, Julia, dear," before noticing their visitor and stopping in her tracks.

"Antonia! What a delicious treat!" Miss Coverley bustled in to give her dearest Duncan's pretty wife a hug and express herself delighted to see her.

"Were you telling Julia about the Drummonds' reception? Oh, I do hope I have not missed too much. Do go on."

Hester tossed aside her pelisse and sat down, eager to be regaled. Antonia glanced at Julia, whose expression conveyed that she should do as she was told, leaving the announcement of Carey's latest betrothal to her. Antonia guessed that Julia wished to tell Hester that news in private and to instruct her not to spread it all over town, as she had cheerfully done with Carey's previous entanglements, not always to Carey's benefit. Hester could become mulish if Julia told her what to do in front of anyone else, family or no.

"Only if you tell me about Lady Jersey's ridotto," Antonia said. "I daresay you chose the more entertaining event to grace with your presence, for indeed, the talk at the Drummonds' was boringly political, and Lord Elgin did not even deign to appear."

She gave the ladies a catalogue of the persons who had attended the reception, as well as a description of the ladies' gowns, the decoration of the house, and the drawings of the marbles on display in the upper gallery.

At this point, as Antonia had guessed, Hester lost interest in the reception and plunged into a lively description of the ridotto, particularly of all the handsome young gentlemen and charming young ladies who had been present. Hester had a knack of knowing even before the persons involved did themselves which lady would make a match with which gentleman, and while she rarely took an active part in bringing about a match herself, she delighted in watching love's progress across the London social scene.

She waited until Hester came to a breathless pause in her narrative before rising and saying she must be off.

"May I drive you somewhere, Aunt Hester? I have no other urgent business."

Julia accepted this assessment of her niece's visit at face value, and Antonia knew then that Elena would find an ally in her. She smiled thankfully at Julia.

"Oh, thank you, dear," Hester gushed. "I should like to go first to Hatchard's to reserve Miss Austen's new book. It is called *Emma*, and I am told that I will quite sympathize with the heroine. But it is quite impossible to obtain a copy from the lending library, so I will have to pay my guinea if I am to read it before it is quite out of fashion . . ."

Chattering happily in this manner, Miss Coverley allowed Lady Kedrington to take her up in her carriage and deposit her in Piccadilly, although she could not persuade dear Antonia to accompany her into Hatchard's and waved good-bye with regret.

"I hope she will forgive me for keeping the news about Carey and Elena from her," Antonia said to her husband that night, after he had come into her room and slipped between the covers with her. "I had no earthly excuse for doing so, except that Julia seemed to wish it."

"Hester never holds a grudge," Duncan said, blowing out

the candle beside the bed. He had listened patiently, as he did every night, to Antonia's recounting of her day's activities, but she knew his signal when he had had enough. And in truth, she was fatigued as well, having spent the time since parting from Hester in ordering provisions for the dinner party for Elena and Carey and in being fitted for a new gown to wear for it.

She persisted a little longer nonetheless. "Have you given any further thought to Elena's odd reaction to that drawing last night?" she asked.

"I expect the mystery will clear itself up one day, if we put our minds to other matters in the meanwhile."

"Excellent advice. I shall put my mind to planning our dinner party to announce Carey's engagement."

"Is this the event that was formerly a soirée?"

"Oh, what does it matter what it is called. It will take place in the evening, and there will be food. You know I never know what to call my little gatherings until someone tells me the next day what they were."

"I thought Julia advised going slowly. Surely, a formal dinner party will put Elena uncomfortably in the center of attention."

"But I would not invite anyone with whom she has not become acquainted—and so she would be among friends."

"Or at least acquaintances."

"I shall introduce her to my friends before that, and so they will be her friends as well."

"Do not exhaust yourself in the cause, my love."

"You always say that, and I never do. You know I enjoy it. Anyway, I shall save my ambitious plans for the wedding."

"You have made up your mind to approve of this match, then?"

"Wholeheartedly—don't you?"

"I bow to your genius in these matters, my love."

She sighed and wondered briefly if her vaunted genius was as dependable as he thought. "Well, I must approve, as my only wish is to see Carey as happy as I am."

He squeezed her hand and reached over in the darkness to kiss her. "Are you happy, Antonia?"

She frowned, then quickly erased it, hoping he had not seen it in the dark. "Of course I am. Do you doubt it?"

He made no reply, but kissed her again, and then again, languidly but relentlessly. Very soon she felt all thought leave her mind, until only sensation remained, and she succumbed again to the wonder of her husband's embrace.

Chapter 4

Dissatisfied with the mere representations of Lord Elgin's marbles on display at the Drummonds' reception, the Kedringtons resolved to visit the real thing as soon as possible. This proved to be several days after the reception, during which time Mr. Fairfax had brought Miss Melville to the house several times, and Lady Kedrington was encouraged to believe that she was becoming comfortable in their company.

"I thought you'd seen the collection," the viscount remarked as he waited for his wife to choose between a green-and-white striped walking dress that she confessed was perhaps a little young for her, and an amber crepe afternoon dress that made her, she feared, look perhaps a trifle matronly.

"You are a young matron," Kedrington pointed out, "so either should be suitable, if unoriginal. Why don't you wear that Prussian blue dazzler I saw being delivered the other day? It looked delightfully unsuitable."

"I'd forgotten that!" Antonia exclaimed, tossing the crepe onto the bed. When Duncan was on hand to assist her to dress, she dismissed her maid, although Betty knew that it would be her duty later to gather up the remains. "And it will be just the thing for our drive in the park afterward." She pulled out the blue dress and held it up in front of her.

"I trust that Miss Melville has been informed of that part of today's treat," Kedrington said.

Antonia looked offended. "You don't think I would really spring something disagreeable on her without warning, do you? Besides, it won't be disagreeable. It's a lovely day for a drive, and she will be with us the whole time. She need not even speak to anyone else, but it will give her an opportunity to see people we might talk about but whom she does not know."

Kedrington muttered something about people he would rather *not* know, but Antonia ignored him.

"It's been an age since I saw the marbles," she said instead, from within the blue silk dress as she dropped it over her head. "You remember, you took me to them when they were still in Park Lane."

Kedrington rose and helped her arrange herself, then did up the fastenings in the back of her gown. "Did I? Then perhaps you will be good enough to explain why we are going again."

"Elena has not seen them."

"Oh."

Antonia paused in her contemplation of her own reflection in her mirror to assess her husband's. "What did you really think of her, Duncan? I vow, when you wish to keep your opinions hidden, you are remarkably adept at it. Even I cannot tell by looking at you what you are thinking. I wish you would teach me to do that."

"Half your charm, my dear, is your artlessness," he said, smoothing the loose strands of hair that disturbed her neckline. "I should dislike putting a damper on it by encouraging you to imitate me. I was trained to it, in any case."

"You mean all that skulking about Spain for the Duke."

He laughed. "You could put it that way—although not in front of the Duke, if you please. As for Miss Melville, I thought her an interesting, intelligent girl, handsome for those who appreciate the type—which I hasten to say I do, although purely in the most academic way. She may well grow into greater beauty with age."

Antonia was ransacking her glove box for an appropriate

pair to go with the blue dress and said absently, "Who may?"

"Miss Melville. Isn't that whom you asked me about?"

"Oh, yes. I was distracted by your skulking. I didn't know you classified women by type. How disappointingly masculine of you."

He turned her toward him and adjusted the dress in front. "I cling to only one type, my love—full-blown roses with blue petals."

He kissed her forehead, but she moved her head before he reached her mouth. "Is that so? What about that honeysuckle vine who clung to you at the Drummonds' reception?"

"She only wanted to hear about my martial exploits."

Having collected Elena at her home—necessitating a detour to the far reaches of Marylebone, of which the viscount's coachman expressed his disapproval by sitting even more stiffly upright at his post than normally—the Kedringtons, Mr. Fairfax, and Miss Melville duly found themselves standing inside the great stone gateway of Burlington House, wondering what to do next, as there was no indication of where, in or out of the building, the marbles were being exhibited, nor was there anyone present who might serve as a guide. Antonia turned to her husband.

"You did say that Lord George had told you to go in the front gate?"

Burlington House had been sold the year before, and the new occupants were apparently not yet settled in.

"Rap on the floor with your cane, Duncan," Carey suggested. "That usually brings the troops to attention."

Kedrington gave him a quelling look and said that as the marbles were reportedly being kept in a separate building on the grounds, he did not suppose the owner would object to their simply strolling in.

"I daresay the staff has not been instructed to escort stray visitors to the display," he said as if, had it been his staff, heads would have rolled. "Let us walk around to the yard," he suggested.

The party were about to suit the action to the word when footsteps were heard coming in their direction from the colonnade to their left.

"Hallo!" said Carey. "Here's rescue perhaps."

"Perhaps not," Kedrington said, listening more carefully. "It's a man with a limp."

The man in question appeared just then from around a pillar and came to a stop, looking mildly startled to see anyone there and even more startled when he recognized one of the fashionable group poised in the forecourt.

"Duncan!"

"Robin Campbell, by all that's holy! What are you doing here?" the viscount said, stepping forward to shake the hand of the pleasant-looking young man who smiled warmly at Kedrington, then at the others.

"Carey Fairfax as well!" he exclaimed. "A happy surprise!"

Antonia's assumption that Mr. Campbell was an army acquaintance of her husband and brother and that he had acquired his limp in the Spanish campaign shortly proved accurate when introductions were made.

Further examination revealed, mainly by the tightness around the former lieutenant's blue eyes, that he had suffered from his wound—or perhaps from the war in general. Antonia had lately noticed more and more of this effect now that the last stragglers were coming home from France—those wounded men whose recovery had meant months in some foreign bed or simply months of delaying the return home that might turn out to be less joyful or less healing than they had perhaps anticipated over the long years of their absence.

Mr. Campbell explained that he had been hired as caretaker of the marbles and overseer of the move to their new home in Bloomsbury, which had been authorized as soon as the bill had been passed for their purchase.

"It's not as grand a job as it sounds," he explained, "re-

ally just glorified guard duty, but it keeps me out of taverns
and doss houses."

He smiled, but Antonia suspected that it was not such a
joke as his wry smile was intended to convey. She decided
that she liked Mr. Campbell, and despite Kedrington's teasing about her predilection for widows and orphans and
other helpless creatures, she would make a friend of Robin
Campbell if she could.

"Can you give us a tour, Mr. Campbell?" she asked him.
"That is, if we are not imposing upon past friendship to
make you break the rules."

"Not at all," said Mr. Campbell graciously. "If you will
follow me?" He offered his arm to Lady Kedrington, who
accepted it with a saucy look back at her husband, and led
her around the colonnade into a space that was apparently
once the yard but was now occupied by a large shed. Carey
and Elena, with Kedrington bringing up the rear, stopped
beside them.

They entered the unprepossessing building and stood
awestruck by the sight of the sculptures—confined there,
Antonia thought fancifully, like ancient gods chained to the
wall of some dark cavern. Mr. Campbell was silent for a
few moments, allowing them to study the figures and form
their own first impressions. Antonia, having seen them before, instead watched Elena, who said nothing, but approached the figures with awe. She reached out to lay her
hand on the smooth marble head of a horse; then she closed
her eyes, as if the touch conveyed something to her. Antonia imagined that she could feel the sun of Greece through
that contact with the taut muscles of that vital, almost living
creature.

"As you can see," Mr. Campbell began at last, just
loudly enough so that the entire party could hear, but addressing himself to Antonia, "this is scarcely the ideal setting. The lighting is unreliable, as we depend still on
natural light from the overhead windows. Gas lighting will
be installed at Montagu House, however, before the official opening ceremonies, and placards describing the

pieces will be affixed so that amateur guides like me will not be necessary."

Antonia transferred her gaze to her guide, assuming an expression of intense interest in his narrative as an excuse to study him more closely.

"I'm sure you know a great deal about the statues and their history—not to mention the controversy surrounding them," she said when he paused to lead them to the next grouping. "But tell me, Mr. Campbell, do you find them beautiful? Are they works of art, and was all this fuss about their acquisition worth it?"

He thought about that for a moment. "It's odd," he said, gazing around as if for the first time, "that people so rarely speak of their intrinsic value. The marbles are looked upon as symbols of one sort or another, but rarely as objects of beauty. And yes, I find them beautiful. Sometimes, in the middle of the night, when there is no one else here, I simply sit and look at them. The poses are various, some belligerent or strained or filled with tension, but they are all somehow restful."

His voice had dropped so that only Antonia could hear him now, but only she might have understood. "All true works of art are restful," she observed, "no matter how violent or distasteful the subject matter. Do you not agree, Mr. Campbell?"

He smiled down at her. "I do, but you would be amazed at the snippets of conversation I overhear about them. Everything from dowagers who are shocked—but vastly entertained—by the figures' lack of decency, to young ladies who contrive to find their beaux' features in the faces."

Antonia giggled. "Do they then speculate on what other features might resemble those of their swains?"

"Lady Kedrington!" Mr. Campbell exclaimed, pretending shock. "How unworthy of you!"

"Oh, Duncan will tell you I have a wayward imagination," she said, laughing. "But no—perhaps you had better not ask him. He will think I am trying to corrupt you."

"Please feel free to try," he urged her, and Antonia was pleased to see that the smile in Mr. Campbell's eyes was freer now, and the lines around them had softened just a touch. He could not be more than thirty, she thought, but old enough to believe he might never make any mark with his life—perhaps even to wonder if he should have left it in Spain.

They walked down the long side of the building, where the remains of the famed east pediment figures were arranged in all the glory of their original positioning on the Parthenon. Mr. Campbell waved his arm grandly at the display, but then spoiled the effect by saying that there were more pieces in another shed attached to the larger one, including some dozen sculptures and slightly more metopes, which he explained were marble squares that formerly separated the parts of a frieze.

As they walked, Mr. Campbell kept up his learned commentary, which Antonia reflected she would have been grateful for on the occasion of her first look at the sculptures, when they all looked so much alike that she was unable to appreciate their variety. Mr. Campbell also offered his personal opinions of the various pieces, and Antonia was most interested in those, for he had apparently studied them in detail and offered a perspective she had not considered previously.

"Notice, for example, the naturalness of the figure's position here," he said at one point. "The muscles of the shoulder work just as they do when a man puts his arm to work in that fashion. You may know that a boxer was brought in once to compare his anatomy to those depicted here, but while the sculptures proved anatomically accurate, they were at the same time strangely more graceful than nature. That, I believe, is what defines art."

Kedrington rejoined them at that point and listened with interest, interrupting only with occasional questions, while Carey and Elena drifted off toward the other side of the room, abandoning their interest in ancient art for absorption in each other. After a short time, however, an exclamation from Elena attracted Antonia's notice, and she turned to see that another man had entered the building, apparently by a side door. Elena walked swiftly toward him and kissed his cheek; Carey, coming up behind her, bowed politely and shook the man's hand.

"Who is that?" she whispered to Kedrington, who responded, "Her guardian, one would assume."

This proved to be the case, as Elena immediately brought Arthur Melville over to be introduced. He was a tall, severely handsome man with graying hair and an air of being not altogether at home in his clothes, which were nonetheless complete to a shade, as Carey would have put it. His posture and manners were overly formal, and Antonia thought he would be difficult to put at his ease, if indeed he ever was in company. A man more different from her last new acquaintance, the personable Mr. Campbell, she could not imagine.

"I am pleased to meet you, sir," she said nonetheless, shaking his hand. "We have become quite fond of Elena already, and it is more than time that we met the rest of her family."

"Her family . . . ? Of course, you speak figuratively," Mr. Melville replied, smiling indulgently at his ward and confirming Antonia in her impression that Mr. Melville was not a kindred spirit. "I do see myself as in some sort an uncle to Elena—a kindly one, I trust. But I wanted to meet you as well, my lady, and when I saw you enter the building, I made so bold as to follow you in."

"How fortunate that you were passing at that moment," Kedrington remarked.

"Not at all. In fact, I . . . er, own some property in this neighborhood and was consulting with my architect about some little renovations when I observed you from the window."

And hurried home to change his clothes, Antonia suspected. She glanced at her husband, but he had assumed the bland air which he wore on occasions of unavoidable tedium—or when he expected his wife to do something outrageous and wished to disassociate himself from her. She wondered which he thought it would be today. Mr. Melville was a trifle fawning, but not quite to the point of tedium. His manners were, indeed, unexceptional; Kedrington would probably tell her that her tendency to informality made her too critical of those who were punctilious to any degree greater than her own.

They continued their tour, Mr. Melville attaching himself to Lady Kedrington. She cast a reproachful glance at Mr. Campbell for allowing himself to be usurped, but he could only return an apologetic shrug as he fell in with Kedrington. Antonia hoped her husband would think to invite his friend to dinner. She supposed they must invite Mr. Melville as well—but preferably not at the same time.

Anticipating her wishes, Kedrington extended an invitation to Mr. Campbell for the following evening, while Mr. Melville was distracted by his conversation with Antonia; he would leave it to her to manage Melville, an easy feat for her. Robin gratefully accepted the invitation.

"Where are you living?" Kedrington asked, half expecting to hear that he was camped out in some corner of Burlington House. Happily, this was not the case.

"A group of us veterans are making use of the family home of Sergeant Hollister, whom you may recall. It turned out that he's something of a nob and could have purchased a commission, although he claims he preferred sticking by his mates. The family made a killing in trade with the Indies over the last century, and although the house is in the East End, it's a bloody great place, where five extra of us are hardly noticed."

"Perhaps I should have invited myself to dine *there*."

Robin laughed. "You're welcome, of course, but it's pretty much like an army mess—scarcely elegant dining at the best of times. In fact, I'm not at all sure I'll remember my manners when I come to you, having used them so little of late."

"Oh, Antonia won't mind, as I'm sure you've noticed."

"You're a lucky dog, Kedrington."

The viscount smiled. "People do keep pointing out the obvious."

He paused just then in his perusal of a huge frieze, having noticed that it was placed on a wheeled platform. Robin following his gaze and explained, "Some of the smaller pieces have already been moved to Montagu House. The larger ones will be taken one by one, most likely at night when their progress will not disrupt traffic between here and there. This frieze will be the next piece to go."

"It doesn't look very secure."

"Oh, it won't be wheeled all the way to Bloomsbury like that. It will be battened down more properly before we go."

"I did not mean precisely that . . . Are any precautions being taken against thieves?"

"Not really. The assumption is that the remaining pieces are all too heavy to move even one of them without a great deal of commotion and several men, and there is a round-the-clock watch on them. I am only one of many guards."

"There has been no vandalism of any kind?"

"Not that anyone has noticed."

"Are you armed?"

Robin began to look concerned. "No."

"I'll lend you something suitable when you come to dinner tomorrow."

"Look, Duncan, do you really think there's any danger?"

Kedrington shrugged. "Very likely not. Put it down to overcaution on my part—or perhaps just a distrustful nature. We all got into bad habits in the war, didn't we?"

Robin smiled, put slightly more at ease. "Some of them come in useful in civilian life, I've noticed."

"Such as esprit de corps, perhaps?" When Robin did not meet his eyes, Kedrington went on, "I refer of course to your current living arrangements. Any other collection of such mismatched individuals would come to blows within days, had they not a strong common history."

Robin smiled and admitted that this was true.

"It also tends to foster trust among comrades," Kedrington went on, closing his net. "So that when one man needs a favor, he will not hesitate to ask to ask another for it."

Robin met his look then, conceding the point. "I'll keep that in mind. Thank you."

Chapter 5

~

"Oh, there you are, Duncan," said Lady Kedrington. "I must thank you for inviting Mr. Campbell to dinner tonight. Carey is taking Elena to the theater—happily, there is some famous Greek tragedy being enacted at Drury Lane—and therefore I need not invite Mr. Melville, and we may have a pleasant evening amongst ourselves."

Kedrington kissed the top of his wife's head and then stepped back to regard her quizzically. She was seated at her writing desk, pen in hand and engagement calendar before her, looking the picture of a society hostess in a white cap and a morning dress of striped India muslin, with a lace fichu tied over her shoulders.

"If I understand you correctly," he ventured, "I have been lucky to choose tonight to invite Robin to dinner, as Elena will not be with us and you therefore need not invite her guardian to bore us at dinner."

"Isn't that what I said?"

"I'm sure you intended to, but occasionally I must test myself to see if I can still interpret your meaning without translation."

She smiled and rose to kiss his cheek. "I am sure we are as much in harmony as we ever were, my love."

"I do have some difficulty in comprehending, however, why a Greek tragedy should cause you happiness."

She pushed him away in mock exasperation. "Oh, you know what I meant."

"I'm afraid I do—which is what concerns me. Will my fame as a man of mystery degenerate into only a reputation for being obtuse?"

"What do you need with mystery when you have something much more fascinating?"

He smiled. "And what may that be?"

"Me, of course."

He smiled and lifted her hand to kiss it. "I hope you will not seduce poor Robin."

"If I have not already brought him under my spell, I shall be very disappointed in myself. But no matter. I mean to introduce him to some nice girl—"

"Not tonight, I trust."

"Oh, no. I must find one first, and they are not so thick on the ground as you might suppose for someone like Robin. I shall consult your aunts, I think."

"I must extend my sympathies to Robin."

"You must not say anything to him, of course. I do not want him to think I am interfering."

"Heaven forbid. Have you presented Elena to Julia, by the way?"

"She passed that hurdle yesterday, which is why I made no objection to her going to the theater tonight with Carey, unchaperoned. She will be much happier if she feels she is not under scrutiny for at least one evening, and Julia will hear about it before I am obliged to tell her myself. Where are you going, by the way?"

"First to call on Julia, before I fall to the depths of her contempt, then to bring Robin here for dinner."

"Surely you need not leave so soon for that. Besides, he would not expect you to come yourself, only to send a carriage."

"I should like to meet some of the fellows he is staying with. I may know some of them."

Antonia eyed him warily. "You will return sober, won't you?"

"I assure you, I will behave myself."

"See that you do. I shall demand a full report from Mr. Campbell on your return—and do not be late!"

Kedrington spent half an hour in his aunts' company, which was passed as usual by Julia's not always subtle reminders to him that he was the head of the family and should comport himself as such. As this conviction was stated whether he had been found lacking in his duty or not, he took it in good part, parrying every statement of hers with a teasing compliment on her cap—which she dismissed with a sniff—or praise of her great-nephew Angus, Kedrington's heir—which never failed to raise her dander, even when she knew perfectly well that he was teasing.

Hester, meanwhile, tried with little success to stifle her giggles at what she knew was his attempt to prevent Julia from endowing her favorite nephew with responsibilities he did not want and to turn his visits into something more like an ordinary afternoon call. Hester would never dare to speak to Julia the way Kedrington did, but she enjoyed listening to him. And, she had told him once in confidence, she believed he was actually wearing Julia down.

Kedrington was still smiling when he left his aunts' house and set his horses in the direction of the City, but navigation of the narrow, crowded streets off Whitechapel Road soon concentrated his attention on his driving and his anxious groom's on the likelihood that desperate footpads might spring from every alley they passed.

"Calm down, Thomas. We are armed."

"Yes, my lord," said Thomas, looking as if he thought an escort of artillery would be insufficient. A beer wagon rumbled noisily out of a side street behind them, and Thomas looked back in alarm.

"And when we get there," Kedrington said, "you are not to call me 'my lord,' if you please. And do not boast to the stable lads about your noble employer, either."

"No, sir."

Kedrington smiled. Thomas was a bright lad and caught

on quickly, even if he was sometimes as nervous as a highly bred horse being asked to charge cannon.

Robin had told him that Hollister's house was in Leman Street, one of the few in the district that boasted large, prosperous homes. Robin had told him that his cattle would be safe in the stables at Number 68, so Kedrington drove through the gate without hesitation, noting that holes in the drive had been patched recently, and the house itself was being repainted.

His arrival did not go unnoticed, and he had scarcely handed the reins to Thomas to stable the horses when Robin and his host came out to greet him. Hollister was a tall man with a ruddy complexion and the large hands of a manual laborer, but his manner was confident without being arrogant, and he spoke like a well-educated man.

Robin clapped Kedrington on the shoulder, saying, "Well, Duncan, I'm glad to see you again. You remember Sergeant Hollister?"

Hollister shook his hand. "Didn't have any trouble finding the way, then, my lord?"

"Not in the least," Kedrington said, taking the ex-sergeant's big hand in his. "Good to see you again, Jim. And please do not put titles between us."

"I didn't mention it to the other men," Robin said, "although some of them may remember you."

"At least by reputation," Hollister put in. He had a ready smile, too, although from what Kedrington remembered, his manner had been somewhat freer in Spain. Doubtless the sergeant's family, much as Kedrington's own, had pointed out the impropriety of a man of substance maintaining the acquaintance of such unsuitable persons as former soldiers of no rank and no position at home. He hoped the sergeant would not be unduly influenced by such opinions.

As if reading his mind, Robin said as they entered the house by a side door, "Jim's family don't live here anymore, having found more genteel domicile on the other side of the city in Kensington."

"Aye," said Hollister, "and a great relief it is. I miss my sisters, but my cousins are a rum lot, and Uncle Jeremiah hasn't forgiven my dad for leaving the business to me—and me for coming back from the war in one piece."

"What sort of business is it, Jim?"

"Carting and general hauling," Jim replied. "What with the way the city's expanding since the war, there's plenty of profit in it. We haul everything from my family's household goods to produce for Covent Garden market. I've been able to hire some of the lads who've come home looking for work, too, which gives me a good deal of satisfaction."

Kedrington hoped that Hollister profited from his generosity in more material ways as well, but he did not make an issue of the sergeant's good deeds. Men of his kind rarely wanted praise for something that they considered to be no effort on their part. Instead, he asked more pertinent questions about the business, thinking to send some custom Hollister's way.

Jim led them to a large room, which must once have been the principal drawing room of the house, or even two, for it extended the length of the building on one side and now served as a kind of club where the men who lived there could smoke, read, and play cards. Half a dozen or so were there now, and Kedrington was introduced to them all as Duncan Heywood.

"You look familiar," one Private Lincoln remarked, sizing Kedrington up. "Been in the army?"

"I'm afraid not."

"Not officially," Robin remarked with a grin.

"Blimey, 'e's a bleedin' diplomat!" exclaimed one man, making everyone, including Kedrington, laugh.

"I've got it!" Lincoln said. "You were with the *guerilleros*! Saw you talking to Old Hooky once at Salamanca. They told me you were an Englishman, though I didn't believe it at the time. You dressed more like a Spaniard then, but you've still got the look of one."

This aroused the interest of the other men present, and despite Kedrington's best efforts, tales of his exploits in

Spain were resurrected and told again. He insisted that most of what they had heard was pure fabrication, but what truth he would admit to shortly won him the respect of the men whose lives might even have been in his hands once or twice. Their friendship would be more hardly won, Kedrington knew, but he could be patient in a worthwhile cause.

"Have a smoke?" Lincoln said, offering a cigar.

"Have one of mine," Kedrington said, producing his Spanish cigarillos. These proved most welcome, and Hollister suggested that he go into the import business.

"Not a bad idea," Kedrington conceded. "If I find a supplier, sergeant, can you market them?"

Hollister grinned. "I reckon we could find more than enough buyers by word of mouth—if we tell these lads here when we get a shipment in."

"Don't suppose you could lay in some *vinho verde*, too, Hollister, eh?" another man offered, to an immediate chorus of groans at the memory of the cheap Portuguese wine they had all been reduced to on the campaign.

It was several hours before Kedrington reminded Robin that they must not be late for dinner, or Antonia would feed them both on the back stoop like beggars. Robin was not reluctant to tear himself away for such a good cause, so they made their farewells, Kedrington promising to come back again.

The sun was close to setting as they drove westward again, and Thomas was even more anxious with every dark alley they passed. Kedrington had learned to ignore him, but Robin was amused by the groom's attempt to imitate his employer's insouciance while casting fearful glances in all directions, and it was he who saw what Thomas did before Kedrington became aware of anything but his horses.

"My lord—"

"Duncan, stop! Something's happening there."

Robin jumped down almost before Kedrington was able to halt his horses, and hobbled down a narrow lane shouting, "Ho, you there! What are you doing?"

"Blast!" said Kedrington. "Here, Thomas, stir yourself and take the horses' heads. Here's a pistol, but for God's sake, don't shoot my best cattle!"

He followed Robin into the lane and found him confronting two thugs with his walking stick. They did not, he was relieved to see, carry pistols, but the knife one of them held and the size of the other's fists were sufficiently formidable weapons. Behind the two, a man lay on the ground, moaning, but Kedrington could see no more than that he was younger and smaller than the other two.

"Bloody 'ell!" said the thinner man, backing up until the wall stopped him. "It's 'is bleedin' ludship!"

"Shaddup!" the big man hissed. "It ain't 'im. It's some other nob."

"Well, what's 'e doin' 'ere, then?"

Kedrington approached the larger man slowly, with an amiable smile and his hands spread out to show that he meant no harm.

"Now, why don't you gentlemen just take yourselves off before you really hurt someone. We won't turn you in if you assure me that you had nothing to do with the plight of the poor fellow on the ground there. What do you say?"

The larger man apparently had nothing to say, for he only grunted and lunged for Kedrington, who easily side-stepped his charge. He delivered a swift blow to the back of the man's head as he went by, unable to halt his momentum, and the thug fell to the ground, silent once more.

The other man's eyes grew wide in the dim light. "Bloody 'ell!" he muttered again. Then, slipping past Robin, he fled down the lane away from them.

Kedrington knelt beside the fallen man and turned him over, but that groan had been his last utterance. He was dead. Searching the man's pockets for some identification, he found only a few coins, one of which was a gold guinea, and what appeared to be a house key. He pocketed this surreptitiously and rose to his feet.

"We can't help him, I'm afraid."

"What will we do with him?"

"Leave him. I'll send Thomas to Bow Street to report the incident, and we'll have to hope they get here before he's stripped bare."

"What was all that about a lordship, do you suppose?" Robin asked as they walked back to their vehicle.

"I don't know," Kedrington said. "But I confess to finding it most curious. I'll think about it."

"So will I, by God!"

They reached the curricle, and Kedrington took the reins from Thomas, who quickly scrambled back up onto the rear of the vehicle. Kedrington looked up at him, then said to Robin, "On second thought, I shall drop Thomas at Bow Street myself. It isn't much out of our way."

The next ten minutes were spent in drilling Thomas as to what he was to report to the magistrate and making him repeat it, including the location of the incident, so that in his nervousness he would not forget it all before he got the story out. They left him there with the viscount's card as an entrée and sufficient cash to take a hackney back to Brook Street, and set off again at once.

"Will we be late after all?" Robin asked, hanging on to the sides of the curricle.

"I think not," Kedrington said as he took a corner smoothly and bowled down Oxford Street. "But there will be no time to spare. Is my cravat straight?"

Robin smiled. "Not a fold out of place."

They did in fact arrive with five minutes to spare to eight o'clock. Robin was fascinated to see his fearless friend turn into an unexceptional, even ordinary, doting husband the moment he entered the house and kissed his wife in greeting.

"Well, my dears, I had nearly given you up," Antonia said, shaking Robin's hand. "But here you are just in time to sit down at the table. Trotter had begun to fret, I can tell you."

Trotter neither confirmed nor denied this as he took the gentlemen's hats, and Kedrington smiled at his wife. "You, of course, were not in the least concerned."

"Why, no—that is what we hire servants for. But now that you mention it," she said, taking her husband's arm, "what *have* you been up to all afternoon?"

"Oh, nothing very interesting," Kedrington said. "Just reliving old times, you know."

Robin grinned and followed them into the dining room. Old times, indeed.

Chapter 6

❧

Lady Kedrington glanced out the library window, saw that the warm afternoon would linger into a fine evening, and went back to arranging profusions of spring flowers in a silver bowl on a side table. It was only one of many such arrangements scattered throughout the house, for, as she had sensibly pointed out to her husband when he raised an eyebrow at the stream of blooms being carted in from the florist's wagon, there was nothing like flowers to accentuate a happy occasion. Furthermore, she had every intention of showing Elena all around the house so that she would feel at home in it, and she wanted every room to look its best for her future sister-in-law.

"Were there not sufficient quantities of tulips at Wyckham *and* Windeshiem to satisfy your requirements?" his lordship inquired mildly from his chair, where he was perusing the morning's post.

"As a matter of fact, there were not," his lady informed him. "I really must speak to Robinson when we are next at home about planting more bulbs."

"We shall be there before you know it," Kedrington said. It was indeed their habit to retire to their country estate by the end of July, after taking a short holiday in some seaside town, preferably not Brighton, which could be more trying than London when the Prince Regent was in residence.

Antonia glanced at him. "Do not think, dearest, that I miss Windeshiem so much as all that. I know I am a country girl at heart, but with all that is going on in town just now, I cannot be sorry to be here in the midst of it."

"I know that your delight in arranging a social affair is forever at war with your desire for a comfortably rural life."

"It is contradictory of me, is it not? You are a treasure, Duncan, to be forever patient with my contradictions."

"For purely selfish reasons, I assure you. It keeps me on my toes to anticipate your next whim—that is, your pleasure."

"*Whim* is the correct word. I do not deny it. I daresay one day you will tire of my flightiness, but so long as you find it novel, I will take advantage of your peculiar fascination."

His lordship smiled and went back to his letters. "Here is one for you, Antonia. Trotter must have overlooked it when he sorted our correspondence."

Antonia took the letter and tore it open carelessly. "It is from your Aunt Hester, confirming her attendance at dinner tonight."

"Julia, one gathers, expects Miss Melville to wait upon her, as the rest of us are obliged to do, now that she has approved her entry into the family."

"Of course, and I cannot say I am sorry for Julia's absence. It was all I could do to whittle down the guest list to a number that would not cause Elena to blanch at seeing them all gathered at the same dinner table."

"Yes, I noticed that your little soirée turned into a dinner party almost overnight. What is the final tally?"

"Twelve. I did attempt to limit the number to six—Carey and Elena, you and I, Hester, and Arthur Melville—but then there would have been no one to make an announcement *to*. You don't think Elena will be overwhelmed, do you?"

"I can only congratulate you on your restraint."

"I did my best to keep the menu simple and drew the line at inviting only those persons who are residing in town, although I should have liked to have Octavian and Isabel to complete the family."

"A wise distinction." Kedrington glanced at his wife speculatively. "How is Isabel?"

Antonia's niece, her late older brother's only child, was in the family way only six months after her wedding, and while Kedrington knew that Antonia was as happy for her as she could be, he did not doubt she harbored a certain envy at the apparent ease with which her niece, only eight years younger than herself, was blossoming into mother-hood. He hoped Antonia would not have much longer to wait. He wished he could alleviate that particular longing of hers; however, he did not attempt any such platitudes as as-suring her that he would always love her whether she gave him an heir or not. It was true, but that did not mean she would believe him.

"Blooming, according to her latest letter. Perhaps I should have included Mr. Campbell," Antonia went on, ap-parently unafflicted by such thoughts as troubled her hus-band. "Elena seemed at ease with him."

"Nonetheless, they are virtual strangers."

"That is true." Antonia sighed and bent to kiss her hus-band's forehead. "And the announcement will appear in the *Times* tomorrow morning. We can always wave it about or post it on the door by way of official announcement." She gathered up her gardening shears and said, "I shall leave you to your correspondence, dearest. I must see if the berries for the sweet course have arrived."

With a smile and a gay little wave, Antonia left the li-brary and closed the door softly behind her. The instant she heard it click shut, however, she took in a deep breath and snatched a handkerchief out of her sleeve to wipe away the tears that welled up despite her determination not to let them.

"Do stop being so foolish," she told herself in a fierce whisper. "Fretting yourself to flinders will achieve nothing!"

Refusing to dwell on her secret, unreasoning fears about her inadequacies as a wife and the dreadful possibility that she would never be a mother—those doubts would pass, they always did, she *knew* they would—Antonia went off to bedevil the cook, harry the maids, and drive her dresser to distraction. And, as always in the Kedringon household, when it came time for her guests to arrive, Lady Kedrington looked as fresh and lovely as a spring day, the decorations were perfection, and the servants went about their remaining tasks with smiles and giggles, as if they had never been more happy in their work.

His lordship appeared, fresh from the talented hands of his valet and ready to greet his guests ten minutes before anyone was expected. He presented himself for his wife's approval in knee breeches and striped stockings, a beautifully cut dark blue coat, a white waistcoat, and a cravat tied in a style she recognized as his own but to which he refused to put a name.

"You *do* look elegant," Antonia told him, "as always."

"And as always," he replied, "you, my love, look delicious."

"Why, thank you, sir," she said, spreading her skirts in a curtsy that served to show off the supple radiance of her pink satin gown. The amethysts in her ears and at her throat had been a gift from Kedrington on their second wedding anniversary.

"Are you coming down to greet our guests?" she asked him.

"No, I leave that chore in your expert hands. When you need me, send Trotter. He will know where to find me."

Antonia gave him a look he dared not attempt to interpret and, with no further word, swept past him toward the stairs. He surely only imagined her saying, as she disappeared, "Slacker!"

The first of their guests to arrive was, unsurprisingly, Hester Coverley, in a youthful but unusually restrained gown of lavender and white stripes. The moment the door was opened to her, she swept past the butler, hugged Antonia, and snatched off her bonnet.

"You need not hide your bonnet from *us*," Antonia said, laughing. "Although I should not suppose you need it indoors."

"Oh, do forgive me, Antonia, dear. Force of habit, you know. Julia does take on so when I wear what she considers a too frivolous or too expensive hat. I do think this one is quite elegant, though, don't you? It's a real ostrich feather. And I got it for a song, I assure you."

"I'm sure you did," Antonia replied, leading Hester into the drawing room. She thought, but did not say, that she would have expected Hester's modiste to give her a large discount for the sheer volume of business Miss Coverley brought her way.

Hester rattled on for several moments about her activities that day, but it was not long before the knocker sounded again, and Carey was announced. He glanced briefly around the room, said, "Ah—Kedrington's not down yet, I see," and announced that he would go up to fetch his brother-in-law.

He bounded up the stairs, and Antonia sank into a chair, prepared to be regaled with more chatter from Hester.

The arrival of Cloris and Edmund Beaumont, however, provided Hester with a companion even more voluble than she, and the two ladies exchanged gossip while Antonia took Edmund aside to inquire how he did.

Cloris Beaumont, née Beecham, had been a schoolmate of Isabel Fairfax during the year they had spent together at a Bath seminary for young ladies, and she had been the first friend the Fairfax ladies found when they came to London for Isabel's season three years before. A vivacious redhead with green eyes and a sunny disposition, she had declared her intention at that time of marrying for money, and no one was surprised when she did so. It was a cause of much more bemused speculation that she actually loved her husband, a handsome but scarcely dashing gentleman some twenty years her senior. That he adored her remained apparent, not so much from his demeanor toward her as from Clory's constant references to "the Beau," as she called him, always with a slight blush and a proprietary tone.

But while Cloris was an old friend, Edmund was still a

relatively unknown quantity, and Antonia was glad for a few words with him before the rest of their guests arrived.

"How are you this evening, Edmund? I trust the weather has not become too sultry for you."

"Not at all. But then, I am used to the Indian climate. Cloris is eager to leave town, however, and I have engaged a house for the summer in Worthing."

"Not Brighton?" Antonia teased.

He smiled, acknowledging the unmodishness of Worthing. "You would be surprised to know that it was Cloris's choice. She claims to be bored with Brighton and says there is nothing new to do there."

"Does she, indeed!"

"Well, we shall see how long she is diverted by Worthing. I have also engaged rooms in the largest hotel on the Steyne in Brighton for a fortnight in August—as a precaution, you understand."

"And what about you? Do you have a preference?"

"My preference is for a happy wife."

Antonia laughed. "How very obliging a husband you are—I trust Clory is properly appreciative."

"I believe she is," he said, and Antonia realized that she still was not well enough acquainted with him to know if he was being wry, smug, or sure enough of the truth of his statement that he felt no need to embellish it.

Lady Sefton and her son, Lord Molyneaux, were announced then, and Antonia hastened to greet them. Lady Sefton was one of the patronesses of Almack's and—more important in Antonia's eyes—she been kind to a very shy Isabel in her first season. She hoped Maria would be so obliging as to take Elena under her wing as well, even if only to reassure her that she would be accepted on her own merits by Lady Sefton's circle. Elena knew well enough that her connection with the Kedringtons was considered one of these merits, but why should that matter?

She kissed Maria Sefton on both cheeks and shook hands with her son.

"Well, Antonia," Lady Sefton said. "I hear that your latest protégée is a young lady quite out of the ordinary way. May I meet her?"

"She has not yet arrived, but do have a glass of sherry with me, and I will tell you all about her!"

Lady Sefton laughed, said that she supposed Miss Melville was waiting to make a grand entrance, and went along with her hostess to sit in a corner and enjoy a comfortable coze.

Shortly, the last of their guests, Sir William and Lady Overton, who lived in the house across from the Kedringtons, arrived to join the convivial party in the drawing room, and it was nearly time for dinner to be announced before Antonia realized that Miss Melville had not yet arrived.

She made her excuses to go in search of Carey and found him with her husband in the billiard room. Kedrington was concentrating on lining up his next shot, and her brother, a morose look on his face, observed his opponent's skill at the game with the look of a man who knows he will never be as good at something as he hoped.

"Oh, what a good shot, Duncan."

He looked up, smiling. "My dear, you have never taken the least interest in billiards. How do you know it was a good shot?"

"Well, that ball went into the pocket—isn't that the object of the game?"

"It wasn't the ball I *wished* to put into the pocket," he replied, racking his cue.

"Well, how should I know that?" Antonia asked reasonably.

"Is Elena here?" Carey asked hopefully, apparently as eager to call an end to his losing game as to see his beloved.

"No, and that is why I have come. It is nearly eight o'clock, and neither she nor Mr. Melville has arrived. Could something have delayed them?"

Carey glanced at the clock, frowned, and replaced his cue as well. "I had no idea it was so late. You should have come sooner, Tonia. I'll go to Gloucester Place at once. Perhaps I shall meet them on the way."

Suiting the action to the word, he made a hasty exit, leaving the door open behind him. A moment later, the sound of the street door closing broke Antonia from her trance and she turned to find her husband gazing at her, one eyebrow raised quizzically.

"Well, what?" she inquired.

"I only wondered what sort of punishment you mete out to guests who are late for dinner. Or is it only husbands who must bear your wrath?"

"Oh, don't be foolish. Anyway, you weren't late."

"It was a near-run thing. I suspect only Robin's presence the other day saved me from a scolding—or worse, a cold dinner."

"Which reminds me," Antonia said, disregarding this nonsense, "I must see to tonight's meal at once."

After she had taken Trotter aside and told him to hold off announcing dinner for a short time, both Kedringtons returned to their guests, to find them enjoying one another's company with no apparent restlessness to get to their dinner, for which small favor Antonia felt excessively grateful.

She was continually aware of the clock for the next half hour, however, even if her guests were not, and the effort to maintain her equanimity quickly gave her an ache in her neck and a dryness in her throat that finally propelled her into the library to seek relief in a surreptitious glass of brandy.

She had scarcely crossed the hall on her return, however, when the front door opened and Carey came in, looking so unlike his usual cheerful self that Antonia, alarmed, came to an abrupt halt.

Confirming quickly that all the doors leading off the hall were closed, she whispered urgently, "Carey! Whatever is the matter? Are you quite well?"

"She's not coming," her brother informed her in a choked voice. He took a deep breath and handed her a letter. Antonia opened it.

Dearest Carey,

I wish I did not have to tell you this in this way, but I cannot continue to deceive you. I cannot let our engagement continue. I do love you—I did not deceive you about that—but I am not the woman you thought me and I cannot involve you further in my sordid affairs. I can say no more now, but I beg you to forgive me and to believe that whatever pain I may cause you at this moment is no greater than mine on having to cause it.

With all my love,

Elena

Antonia stood perfectly still for several moments, attempting to absorb the meaning of this amazing missive. She failed.

"Carey . . ."

Her brother started, as if he had forgotten she was there and had followed his mind's eye to some other place or time.

"I don't understand, dearest. How has she deceived you? What sordid affairs could she possibly be involved in?"

Carey shrugged, then spoke so quietly that Antonia could scarcely hear him even over the slight murmur of voices penetrating the closed doors around them.

"I don't know . . . I just don't know."

"But . . . but had you no inkling that something was wrong?"

"No. I can only guess . . ."

Antonia stepped closer to her brother and put her arm around his waist. "What, dearest?"

"I can only suppose that she did not really love me . . . at least, not as much as I love her, and she has decided that a clean break will spare my feelings. I always knew she was too good for me, but I had hoped that—"

"Do not say that!" Antonia exclaimed, stepping back and addressing him forcefully. "I know that I am your sister and therefore partial, but I have never denied your little foibles.

Never say you are not worthy of anyone you choose to bestow your affections on. You *are* worthy, Carey, and any girl would be foolish to deny it. Indeed, Elena does not deny it!"

She handed the letter back to him. "See here—she says she loves you, and why should she not? There is something else wrong, and we must simply find out what it is and fix it."

"Fix what?" said Kedrington's voice from behind her. "What's broken?"

"Carey's engagement," Antonia said, handing her husband Elena's letter. "But it is only a stupid misunderstanding that we will resolve in an instant as soon as we speak to Elena."

"She wouldn't see me," Carey said, only slightly less gloomily.

"Well, she will see me," Antonia said with determination. She looked to her husband as if for confirmation and found him gazing at her in admiration.

"Won't she?"

"How could she resist?" he asked rhetorically. "Ah . . . in the meanwhile, my love, what would you like me to tell our guests? Not to mention that their dinner is getting cold."

Antonia considered this for mere seconds. "Fortunately, no one but ourselves knows that an announcement was to be made—except Hester, I suppose, and I will take her aside to explain. Simply tell them that we have just received word that the guest we were still awaiting has suddenly been taken ill and have Trotter announce dinner at once. Come, Carey, let us go upstairs and compose ourselves for a moment. Then there is no reason why we may not enjoy our dinner. Tomorrow is time enough to think about solving this riddle."

Antonia was aware that she continued talking in this manner more to convince herself than her brother, but Carey seemed willing enough to believe her—at least for the time being—and Kedrington obligingly carried out her instructions and returned to their guests, his customary sangfroid revealing no hint that anything was amiss.

If Carey was unusually subdued at dinner, this went nearly unnoticed in the general feeling of camaraderie over a repast of such succulence that it was talked about for a week afterward. Antonia subdued the occasional flashes of self-blame—she should not have asked Elena to face so many strangers, she should have limited the guest list after all, she should not have had the dinner party so soon in the first place—which dimmed her usual smile only momentarily. And Kedrington saw to it that the wines served during and after the meal were of a quality that would not only confirm his generosity as a host but cause his guests to forget any slight irregularities that might show between the cracks in his wife's or brother-in-law's demeanor so as to arouse comment. He was confident that there would be no comment but only praise about this occasion.

Yet when the party finally drew to a close, all their guests had departed, and Carey had taken himself, dispirited but calmer, to bed, Antonia found herself gazing once again at the flowers in the silver bowl by the library window, wondering that they were still so fresh and untouched by the emotional turmoil that had filled the air around them all evening.

She reached out to stroke the petal of a pink rose, but just then her husband came up beside her and covered her outstretched hand with his. She sighed and looked up at him.

"I have been puzzling over that letter all evening," she said, "and I can still not imagine any reason for it."

He was silent for a moment as he stroked her fingers, separating them and running his own up and down the valleys between them. Then he raised her hand to his lips and kissed it lightly.

"Nor can I," he admitted. "But I do agree with you that there is more behind this than a simple feminine change of mind. Elena is not the kind of woman to play fast and loose with a young man's affections, and even if she felt she could not make him happy, I do not believe she would let him down so clumsily."

"Then what are we going to do about it?"

He smiled. "*We?* My sweet, matters of the heart are scarcely my area of expertise. Call on Miss Melville tomorrow, as you said you would, and tell me what transpires. I will give my advice if I have any, but I suspect your feminine instincts will be a far surer guide in this matter."

"Pooh. That is only your way of saying you will not involve yourself."

"Not at all. I am as eager as you to see Carey happily settled. If I can help, I will, but for the moment I can see no way to do so."

Antonia snapped off the pink rose from its stem and held it to her nose briefly while the eyes she turned up to her husband lighted with some of their old mischief.

"I shall find a way, Duncan, never fear."

"I would never doubt it."

Chapter 7

~

"Carey, dearest, I wish you would tell me a little more about your courtship of Miss Melville—if it is not too painful. Perhaps together we may be able to understand why Elena has acted in the way she has."

Lady Kedrington gazed at her brother, wishing she could say all she truly felt. It broke her heart to see Carey so despondent, but Duncan had advised her to give him time to absorb what had happened and only then to offer to help. "Carey is well able to handle his own affairs," he had said, "only give him time to think how to do it."

Time. Antonia looked again at the clock. Although she was eager to call on Miss Melville herself to ask the questions that plagued her, she recognized that even the most socially ambitious of guardians would not open his door to a caller of any rank before noon. She had therefore delayed her brother at the breakfast table long enough to arm herself with as much knowledge as she could gain in pursuit of her objective.

Carey had scarcely slept, as he informed his sister in blunt terms on entering the breakfast room. He was properly dressed, thanks to his stubborn valet, but his light brown hair was already tousled from running his hand through it, and his hazel eyes held nothing like their usual sparkle.

Antonia had promptly poured coffee for him, but he

had refused her offer to fill his plate. After his third cup of coffee, however, he began eyeing Antonia's glazed ham and eggs with renewed interest and finally spoke more than two words in sequence.

"I expect Kedrington was up long ago and has gone out by now," he remarked.

"Yes. I believe he intended to spend the morning at Brooks's—although what he can find at his clubs to entertain him at this hour defeats my imagining. Would you prefer to confide in Duncan, my dear?"

"Confide . . . ? Oh, no . . . you tell each other everything anyway, so telling one of you is the same as telling the other in any case . . ."

His voice drifted away as if carried off by a particularly forceful thought, and Antonia, recognizing its direction, quickly asked, "Is that the sort of . . . of intimacy you felt with Elena?"

"Well, yes . . . at least, I thought so. I certainly told her everything *I* felt, and she listened and never criticized in any way, so I was comfortable with her . . ."

He frowned. Antonia, to give him a moment to collect his thoughts, got up to fetch him some more substantial nourishment from the covered dishes on the sideboard.

"I've thought about it and thought about it since last night, Tonia, and I see now that what you mean by intimacy was all on my side. I never gave her a chance to confide in me, even had she wanted to, and now it's clear to me that she didn't. Why should she want to when she never—"

"Carey, if you are going to say again that Elena does not truly love you, I shall . . . I shall throw this coffee at you, even though it is no longer hot enough to snap you out of this absurd conceit you have fabricated. Why, even Duncan agrees that some outside difficulty we know nothing of must have motivated Elena to call off your engagement. Neither of us has supposed for an instant that her love has cooled, and it is nonsensical for you to think so!"

She sat down again and banged the filled plate on the table in front of him.

Carey smiled at his sister's vehemence. "Thank you, love. Your loyalty will sustain me even if you do turn out to be wrong about Elena."

"I am not wrong. Now stop dwelling upon impossibilities and eat your breakfast. Then tell me what you know about Elena's background—and confine yourself to the facts, as Duncan might say, without any emendations. You told me, for example, that Elena is an orphan."

Carey obligingly dug into his food and attempted to answer her questions between bites.

"Her parents are dead, yes. She does have family in Greece, but I believe they are only distant cousins, most of whom she has not seen since she was a child."

"And how did she happen to come to England?"

"She was sent here for her schooling when she was quite young. That was before her parents died—both at once, I gather, in a coaching accident, although I did not wish to press her for details. Melville had met the family in Greece and sponsored her, from a distance at first. He only became her guardian on her parents' deaths."

"When did you meet her, Carey?"

He smiled at that and recounted the inauspicious beginning of their courtship and the scene in the little square.

"I was never so astonished that I seemed suddenly to come into her favor, but I dared not question it for fear of breaking the spell."

Sympathetically, she asked, "And when did you know you loved her?"

He did not seem to mind her asking the question, but confessed, "I'm not precisely sure. At first, it was her air of mystery that was fascinating—she doesn't look or act like any other of the season's beauties, does she? She's certainly not silly, as so many of them are. I never thought I'd fall in love with a girl who doesn't smile all the time and who thinks before she speaks, but I suppose it's true that opposites attract."

"I should be more inclined to say you complement each other."

"Well, she didn't seem to mind that I'm a jack-pudding. I used to—I teased her that she is unromantic, but I can't deny that her differences from other girls intrigued me. She seemed so foreign, so *exotic*. I thought we should have nothing to talk about, but she has been in England a long time, and she has had the usual, if unusual, upbringing, and, well . . ."

"I know. She *listens*."

Carey was silent for a moment, falling into contemplation again. "I wonder if I didn't listen enough to her. There must be something more I could have done, or something I did that I shouldn't have—"

Antonia jumped to her feet at that. "I refuse to listen to a catalogue of your sins of commission and omission, Carey. Come, finish your breakfast while I get my hat. Then let us make our way to Mr. Melville's house before you sink yourself in the dismals again."

Once propelled into action, Mr. Fairfax became more cheerful again, keeping up a running commentary all the way to Gloucester Place. His sister was unsure whether this meant he was viewing the future with more optimism or was merely whistling in the dark. Antonia was convinced, however, that Carey had been disappointed more in himself than by Elena. In his eyes, she had no doubt, Elena could do no wrong. Antonia resolutely silenced the small voice in the back of her mind that said the fault might yet be laid at Miss Melville's door.

"When you see Elena—" she began, when Carey paused for breath. By his startled expression, she saw that he had not contemplated the possibility of actually speaking with her today, but she went on nonetheless.

"—you must say nothing that might cause her to think you blame her for anything. Only tell her you love her, several times if you can contrive it, and speak about your future together as if it were never in doubt. I can assure you, as a romantically minded female myself, that is what she would prefer to hear over all else. It may be hard for her at first, but ultimately your love will win her over."

Carey agreed with a sigh to follow her advice, but he was never to be given the opportunity to do so.

They alighted at the Melville residence, and the door was answered by Arthur Melville himself, which set Antonia back for a moment; she had not supposed the master of this house would be so inconsiderate of the proprieties as to take over his servants' duties, however momentarily. This seemed to occur to Melville, too, when he realized what he had done, and a fleeting expression of annoyance crossed his features before he recomposed them into the countenance of a delighted host.

"Ah, Lady Kedrington, do forgive my informality. It is only that I happened to be passing the door just at the moment when the knocker sounded, and . . . well, do come in, please."

As if to restore the world to its rightful order, Mr. Melville immediately pulled a bell beside the door and presently they were ushered by an imposing butler into an immaculately kept sitting room and offered refreshment.

"I do so regret that Elena is not at home," Mr. Melville said before Antonia had a chance to ask for her. "She has gone into the country to stay with my sister for a short time."

Carey looked crestfallen and immediately fell into a renewed lethargy, flinging one leg over the other and staring out the window, his hand on his chin and his attention anywhere but on the conversation. His former anxious impatience transferred itself to his sister, who disregarded his relapse, being more concerned for the moment with learning about Elena's equally strange behavior of late.

"I'm so sorry," she said solicitously to her host. "I trust Miss Melville is not ill?"

He smiled. "You are very discreet, Lady Kedrington, but I know—at least approximately—the contents of the letter my ward forwarded to your brother last night. When Elena sent word that she would not attend your dinner party, I naturally went immediately to her room to demand an explanation. She would say nothing but that she had decided the match would not suit, and when I said I would go to you anyway and attempt to apologize for her, she begged me not to do so and burst into tears."

Antonia brightened, convinced that tears were a good sign. At least they showed that Elena had not thrown Carey over for any lack of love.

"Did she give no hint that . . . that something was preventing her, against her will, from marrying Carey?"

Mr. Melville shook his head regretfully. "Not a word. And I have racked my brain to think of some reason, to no avail. I even searched my own conscience to learn if I had inadvertently said something . . . but I am reasonably certain that I have conveyed my personal approval of the match. For what it is worth. I fear that in matters of the heart, I have little experience to offer a young girl—nor any authority to compel her in any way."

He was beginning to display the overly modest self-deprecation that Antonia found annoying, so she prodded him in another direction.

"Could it have been some family matter?" she asked. "I beg your pardon, for I know you are in essence her only close family, but I understand there are cousins in Greece . . . ?"

"Oh, she has other family than that. She has a brother—"

That penetrated even Carey's abstraction. He turned his head toward Elena's guardian at the same moment that Antonia exclaimed, "A brother! But how is it that we knew nothing—that is, you do not mean to say that this brother has forbidden the banns!"

"No, no, nothing of the sort! That is, I do not know what his reaction would be to the match. We have heard nothing from Dimitri recently, and I daresay that even if he did not approve, Elena would not let his opposition sway her, since they have been estranged for some years."

This tale was becoming stranger by the word, Antonia thought. Attempting with difficulty to curb her impatience, she said, "But you can imagine some difficulty involving this brother?"

Mr. Melville hesitated, while Carey gripped the arm of his chair in agitation. Antonia put her hand out to cover his and gave him a soothing smile.

"I can only guess," Melville went on finally, "that Elena may fear Dimitri's bringing some disgrace on her or giving Mr. Fairfax—and you, my dear Lady Kedrington—a disgust of her for his sake. He is, you see, an ardent Greek nationalist."

"What the devil does that have to say to anything?" Carey burst out at last. "Kedrington's not in the government, and I don't give a hoot for politics."

"I believe Mr. Melville fears some other kind of scandal," Antonia said quietly, to calm her brother's lacerated nerves. "Is that what you meant, sir?"

"Indeed, yes!" Mr. Melville said, looking considerably hotter under the collar. "I have heard from reliable sources that the nationalists may be planning some sort of demonstration when the Parthenon marbles are moved to their permanent home. Of course, if that is all it amounts to, Elena is doubtless needlessly concerned, but—"

"But fanatics have been known to throw bombs and attack public figures," Carey said.

"Surely not!" Antonia protested. She looked from one of the gentlemen to the other and saw from their expressions that neither of them would have been surprised at some such story appearing in tomorrow's *Times*—with the name of Elena's mysterious brother heavily involved. She promptly vowed to lay the whole puzzle before her husband and solicit his opinion, which was often surprisingly informed. Indeed, it was all she could do to remember to collect the pertinent facts before dashing home to consult with him.

Calling on her last reserves of patience, she asked her host, "Did you say the brother's name is Dimitri? Does he live in London?"

"Dimitri Metaxis. That is Elena's family name, you know, although she was kind enough to adopt my surname when she came to England. I regret I have no notion where he may be living. As I said, we have not seen him for years."

Antonia could see that even Carey was a stranger to the name and wondered what else Elena had not told him. She was in no way swayed from her opinion that Elena loved her brother and that something other than a change in her feelings was at work here, but she knew Carey well enough to know that ferreting out social details was not something it would ever occur to him to do. Perhaps Kedrington could be prevailed upon to help find out more about Dimitri Metaxis. In the meanwhile, she would consult Duncan's aunts about any *on-dits* that might be circulating about mysterious foreigners.

Eager to pursue these avenues toward the truth, Antonia rose, bade good afternoon as graciously as she was able to a bemused Arthur Melville, and dragged her brother determinedly past the door.

"I don't see that all that explains anything," Carey grumbled when they were on their way back to Brook Street. "And I don't believe Elena is in the country. She would have needed to leave very early this morning, and she never mentioned any cousin. We should have demanded to see her."

"We could scarcely have stormed the upper stories of Melville's house in search of her," Antonia pointed out. "And the existence of a country relation of her guardian cannot be a surprise to you, since you apparently did not even know that your betrothed has a brother. Doubtless there is a simple explanation for all this, and I am certain that I—and Duncan—will discover it when we have had a moment to devote some thought to it."

Surprising herself at the coherence of her argument, Antonia fell silent. Carey seemed sufficiently impressed by her plan to make no objection to it, although he shifted in his seat so often and so violently that they had not crossed Oxford Street before his sister was scolding him roundly for wearing bald spots on the expensive leather seat coverings in her best visiting carriage.

When they alighted at the Kedringtons' doorstep, Carey immediately walked off in the direction of Bond Street, saying he was going to Jackson's boxing salon, for he needed to work off his frustrations somehow, and he did not suppose Antonia wanted him pacing his room all afternoon.

Antonia bade him a brief farewell before hurrying into the house and inquiring of the servants about her husband's whereabouts. But again she was doomed to disappointment.

"His lordship went out not half an hour ago," Trotter informed her. "It is my understanding that he received a letter calling him away."

"What letter?" Antonia asked, removing her hat.

"His lordship informed us that dinner should not be held for him," Trotter went on, apparently not hearing this question, "and said that in the event of his being detained longer, he would send word of when he will return."

On her ladyship's further demand to see the letter, Trotter was taken aback, but sent for the viscount's valet, who, taking in Antonia's expression, did not waste time questioning her right to read her husband's mail. Milford did, however, spend some moments locating the letter, while Antonia paced her bedroom, attempting to arrange her thoughts to include Kedrington's unexpected absence. Milford then handed her a crumpled piece of paper, apparently retrieved from his employer's wastepaper basket.

Antonia smoothed out the paper and read:

Dear Kedrington:

Something rather odd is going on here. I should appreciate your advice.

Urgently,

R. Campbell

Antonia sat down inelegantly on her bed, even more mystified than before.

"Well," she said to herself, for Milford had beat a discreet retreat, closing the dressing room door behind him, "it seems I must again be patient."

Chapter 8

L ord Kedrington stood before Iris's graceful marble torso at an angle that permitted him to study the other persons in the large room without drawing attention to himself. He was amused to see that the unassuming building in the rear of Burlington House was fast becoming a popular attraction, for an assortment of persons whom he would not have supposed to be patrons of the arts were present and engaged in animated discussion, some of which he perceived actually to concern the antiquities on display for their admiration.

Kedrington had entered the building through the gardens, thinking to thus avoid being seen, but he was followed almost at once by a gray-haired matron of impressively aquiline features, who was now examining a frieze through her lorgnette and remarking to her companion—a tall, angular young man who might have been a grandson or great-nephew—that she supposed this rather belligerent depiction of warlike figures was intended to symbolize the triumph of Greek civilization. The young man replied in a bored tone that in his estimation it more accurately depicted a civilization whose time was not only long gone but had never reached the heights of Britannic majesty in the present century.

A somewhat less informed young woman in a gown that was more revealing of her charms than was customary for afternoon wear inquired of her friend, similarly attired, which of the statues were the ones that had been lost over-board on their passage to England from Greece. Her friend replied that she believed the lost ones were the subject of Byron's poem "Maid of Athens."

Kedrington was unashamedly listening to the conversation of two gentlemen who appeared to actually have some knowledge of sculpting techniques and the texture of marble when he felt a presence at his back.

"Spying again, eh, Duncan?"

Recognizing the voice, Kedrington smiled. "Merely eavesdropping, my dear Robin—a poor younger cousin of your full-fledged spying."

"But a necessary talent to cultivate as a precursor to more serious espionage, I believe."

Kedrington did not deny it. He turned to face his friend, keeping his back to the room so that they could not be identified, nor their conversation be overheard, by any interested parties. It was perhaps an unnecessary precaution, but Kedrington performed it automatically.

Robin smiled and said, "There is no urgent need for discretion. We may speak in my office."

"You have an office on the premises? I am impressed."

"You will not be when you see the office. However, I should like first to give you a short tour. I know that you have seen all the works already, but indulge me in this, and I shall explain my reasons afterward."

"More and more intriguing. Lead on, Macduff."

Campbell winced. "I wish you would not make such unfortunate allusions."

"Macduff slew a tyrant and was covered in glory."

"But at a cost greater than I would care to pay. I long only for a settled life."

Kedrington studied his friend's expression closely, but the object of his scrutiny must have been aware of it, for he deliberately gave nothing away.

"Yet something has unsettled your life lately."

"Indeed," was Mr. Campbell's only reply.

Leaning lightly on his cane, he led the viscount around

some of the less monumental sculptures, naming each and giving a brief history. Kedrington was at first more interested in observing his friend, who seemed invigorated by whatever complication had entered his life as a result of his position as caretaker of the infamous marbles. However much Robin might wish for a settled life, a part of him, Kedrington suspected, still craved the exhilaration of his army days. Even his limp was less noticeable.

He soon turned his attention to the pieces he was being shown, however, aware that something about them was important in this mysterious matter for which Robin had called on his advice. He tried to look at them in a different way than he had before, and observed their surface textures and other physical features this time over their artistic merit. He ran his hand over several of them, at which gesture he caught Robin looking at him in satisfaction.

"Well, what do you think?" Campbell asked, almost eagerly, a short time later—as if, Kedrington thought, he were an art student who had presented his works for the first time to his master for approbation.

They had now retired to Robin's office, which was, as he had indicated earlier, little more than a glorified pantry. Nonetheless, it boasted two reasonably comfortable chairs and a writing table, as well as a narrow cot and a bookcase that, other than a few volumes of popular reading, contained what looked to be Campbell's mess kit, bedroll, and field telescope. There was also a bottle of brandy. The viscount picked this up.

"Spanish." He glanced at his friend. "Contraband?"

"Not at all. Legitimate spoils of war. Would you care for a glass?"

"Thank you, yes. I accept despite my suspicion that your supply of the stuff is limited because I can, and shall, replace it—out of my spoils, of course."

Robin grinned and pulled two glasses out of his mess kit. At Kedrington's raised brow, he explained, "I *have* acquired some more civilized tools than tin cups and forks since my return—thanks in large part to Hollister, of course."

"I am glad to hear it."

The viscount accepted a filled glass, pulled up one of the chairs, and sat on it, stretching his long legs in front of him.

"Would you care to give me a hint as to what I am supposed to be thinking about?" he said.

Campbell, aware of his friend's facility at keeping two or three trains of thought going at once and pulling one forward while another was in progress, recognized now that he was only belatedly answering his first question.

He sat down, but could not be still. Leaning forward, with his hands on his knees, he announced, "I believe one of those pieces I showed you is a fake. Can you guess which one?"

Kedrington thought for a moment, then said, "The second panel in the frieze that you described as being one of the less damaged pieces because of its sheltered position on the wall of the Parthenon."

Campbell sat back with satisfaction and clapped his hands twice on his knees. "I knew it! I knew I could trust you to spot it. What made you pick that one out, not knowing what you were looking for?"

"I expect that was part of the reason, that I was not looking for anything in particular and so my eyes were open to any possibility. It seemed to me that that panel did not exactly match the ones on either side of it. Also, the stone, while rough, was not weathered in the same way."

He was silent for a moment, but his friend gave him no further explanation of why he had called on him.

"Are you telling me," Kedrington finally ventured, "that the genuine piece has been stolen?"

"That is what I believe."

"But why? And more important, how? It's a relatively small piece, but it would take a great deal of effort and at least several men to move it."

"The why is, as you say, not difficult to imagine. A great many people believe that we—that is, Lord Elgin, but by extension, the British in general —have no right to the marbles and that they should be returned to Greece."

"So you believe Greek patriots may be behind this."

Robin shrugged. "Then again, someone with no loyalty to either side may simply wish to steal them."

"Why? They could not be resold."

"For ransom. The pieces may be hard to move, but they would not need to be guarded and fed."

"Which brings us back to the how," Kedrington mused, sipping lightly at his brandy. "Admittedly, the engineers we had in Spain could move objects as heavy as these fairly quickly, even over rough ground, and anyone with the same skills could, at least in theory, do the same here. But even under cover of darkness, how would they get out of the building unseen, and where would they take the pieces?"

"That is the question I have lain awake nights pondering. I hoped to put your brain to the same problem, since mine is quite weary of it."

"Why don't you consult someone in authority—some member of the board of inquiry, or the museum staff?"

Robin shook his head. "I have been reluctant to bring anyone else in just yet. I've pondered the various possibilities until my head aches. If it turns out that the anti-Elgin faction are not actually behind the theft, knowledge of it might encourage them to greater vociferousness, even if they did not take umbrage at the implied accusation. Not to mention that anyone, myself included, who has regular access to the marbles might come under suspicion. If I were removed from this position, I could do nothing further to locate the piece and prevent any further thefts."

"Is it important to you that you solve this mystery?"

"Yes. It happened on my watch, Duncan. I am not the only guard on duty, but the others are all under my supervision, and I feel responsible."

"Can you vouch for the honesty of all the other guards?"

"I think so. I will, of course, investigate them all again, as discreetly as possible."

Kedrington considered that for a moment, then pulled a pocket notebook out of his coat and made a notation.

"When did you first notice the missing piece?"

"Last night. That is not to say the switch could not have been made days ago, but I generally walk around the entire collection once before I retire, and I believe I would have noticed the change before last evening if it had been done prior to that."

"Have you noticed any suspicious-looking persons lurking about?"

Robin smiled. "You were watching them today when I met you. They *all* look odd to me—although that may be simply because I am inordinately sensitive to oddities today."

"Which reminds me to ask you how all those people got in. Has the collection been opened to the public?"

"Not officially, at least not at this venue." Robin shrugged. "But it has become public knowledge where the stones are being kept, and people simply come in by the garden gate. I posted a guard there, as of today, and he has everyone sign a registry, but that is as much as I have the authority to do."

"Do you recall any visitors before today who seemed to take an unusual interest in that particular frieze?" Kedrington asked. "Or in any of the pieces, for that matter?"

"I recall only a young man who came by himself three or four times but has not returned. He looked as if he might be Greek, but I did not speak to him or overhear him in conversation with anyone else. There were also two fellows who looked as if they worked on the docks and knew nothing about art. They spent only five minutes all told giving the place the once-over."

"Which may very well be precisely what they were doing," Kedrington said, making a note. "Obviously, no one man could have moved that piece, so there must be some kind of gang involved, if only to provide the muscle."

He was silent again for a moment, gazing thoughtfully off into the distance, as if he were not hemmed in closely by four walls. "They would also need an artist, or at least a craftsman, skilled enough to make the forgeries."

His friend snatched at that. "So you do think there may be another theft, that this gang will not stop at one piece?"

Kedrington shrugged. "What use is only one, and not one of the better pieces at that? It has little intrinsic value for purposes of ransom, and less symbolic purpose. For that, they would have taken a more well-known piece—Dionysus, for example. I suspect that this panel was a kind of test, to see if the piece was missed. If it was not, or it seemed that it was not, they might be emboldened to try again. That is why I agree with you about not informing anyone in authority about the theft. Also, if they become emboldened, we may be able to catch them in the act."

"We?"

Kedrington smiled. "I hope you did not seek my opinion only as an academic exercise. Now that you have whetted my curiosity, you must allow me to help solve the puzzle."

Robin looked relieved. "I hoped I would not have to beg for your help, but I must tell you I am tremendously grateful. I do not know what I should have done had you not offered it."

"I daresay you would have thought of something, but perhaps I may speed the process up. We cannot chance the forgery going unnoticed for very long. Once the cat was out of the bag, we would be considerably hampered in our efforts."

"What can I do?"

"First, approach Sergeant Hollister and see if you can recruit some of the men living with him as additional guards, particularly at night."

"That did occur to me, but I'm glad you suggested it."

"Next, lower the light as much as you can on that particular frieze to take wandering eyes away from it."

"Perhaps I could have a scaffold put around it and say a crack has been discovered or some such thing."

Kedrington shook his head. "That would only call more attention to it, and we wish neither the thieves nor the authorities to take a second look. Also, as discreetly as you can, keep an eye on that piece and make note of who looks at it with any special attention."

"Shall I take any of the other guards into my confidence?"

"Not just yet. I will do the investigation you mentioned earlier, since it would be less noticeable if I did it rather than you, and I may have other sources of information."

"I should think that highly likely."

"Don't grant me powers I may not have, dear boy. I was only a fair to middling spy."

"Rubbish. And even if that were true, you have an infinitely wider circle of acquaintance than I and far greater . . . resources."

Kedrington knew very well that his friend referred to his fortune, but knew too that Robin did not resent him for it. Men became his friends in large part because differences of wealth and station meant nothing to them in comparison with compatibility of experience and outlook. He also chose his friends on the basis of their honesty, and he had never doubted Robin Campbell's. If there was any possibility of harm coming to him because of this theft, even if there was never another one, he must do what he could to prevent it.

"I must go now," he said, rising and setting aside his brandy glass. "Antonia will not demand to know where I have been if I contrive to be on time for dinner—as you well know. Later, after she is asleep, I shall return and keep watch with you for a part of the night at least."

"Thank you. That is more than I dared ask, Duncan. But you cannot be here every night."

"I don't intend to be. Tomorrow should be time enough to put some of Hollister's men in place—if they are willing. Or we may be able to inform another of the present guards what is afoot. Have you a key?"

"Eh? Oh, yes. Take mine, for I shan't leave tonight." He took a key down from a nail in the wall concealed behind the bookshelf and handed it to Kedrington. "I'll show you the door it fits."

Kedrington waited only until the doors were closed on the last visitor, at which point he and Campbell made his watchman's rounds together before Robin showed him the back door, to which the key fit, and bade him good night.

"Just a moment," Kedrington said, closing the door again. He reached into his pocket and extracted the key he had found on the body of the victim of the thugs they had interrupted two nights before. He held it next to Robin's key, then tried it in the door. It did not fit.

"Where did you get that key?" Robin asked.

Kedrington smiled. "I'm afraid I robbed a dead man."

"The man we found the other night? Did you find out who he was?"

"Not by name—but that is something else you may ask Hollister. Apparently the man was a former soldier, although not one of those who would have come through Leman Street. Perhaps he can make further inquiries. I'll write down the name of the man at Bow Street whom I took into my confidence. He can give you the few other details there are."

"Do you think he has something to do with . . . all this?"

"Very likely not. It was just a thought." He smiled wryly. "No, it was just a feeling. You remember that prickling you get on the back of your neck just before a surprise attack?"

"All too well."

"It was something like that. Besides, I am curious about the 'lordship' the other men spoke of. I'm sorry now that we didn't hand the big man over to Bow Street ourselves; he might have revealed something."

"Still, that is a puzzle Hollister will be interested to follow. You know how stubborn he is."

"As you say, all too well. However, I think I would rather have his muscle on hand here. Ask him to have some other clever fellow run the dead man to earth."

This agreed to, the two men shook hands.

"Thank you again, Duncan," Robin said as the viscount slipped out into the dusk.

"Nonsense, dear boy. I'm looking forward to the mission!"

Robin grinned. "So am I—now!"

Chapter 9

~

Carey Fairfax sat on a bench in the little square off Gloucester Place where he had first met Elena Melville. Of course, he reminded himself, that had not been their first meeting, but he liked to think of it as such, for he was thus able to forget his earlier, clumsier—not to say embarrassing—efforts to impress her. Now they came back to him all too vividly, and he alternated between fond remembrance and acute self-loathing.

Attempting to redirect his mind toward the future and a more positive outlook, he glanced up at the corner of Elena's house, which was visible to him through the trees. He did not think she could see him from the house, and therefore it was not knowledge of his presence that prevented her from venturing out. Carey had earlier ridden his horse up and down the street, but when dustmen and fruit vendors began hailing him familiarly, he had given this up as being overly conspicuous.

He had then begun a circuit of the square and the nearby streets on foot. That had the advantage of his being able to converse with the same vendors and street workers, and since he enjoyed talking to all sorts of people, even when he was not feeling particularly gregarious, it was not long before they were all aware of his sad story and wished him the best of luck in winning back his lady.

But he had not yet contrived to see Elena in order to begin to attempt to do so.

Surely, she must leave the house sometime. Was there possibly another door of whose existence he was unaware? He did not suppose she would go out by the kitchen, unless she knew he was lying in wait for her, and in that case, she should be more likely not to go out at all. He realized that he had very little familiarity with Elena's habits and her daily activities when he was not with her to suggest them.

He was gazing at the upper stories again when a voice said, " 'Ullo, luv. No luck yet?"

"Oh, Mary. How do you do? No, I'm afraid I've not seen Miss Melville yet."

The pert, round-faced little flower seller with whose father—the proud possessor of his own cart—Carey had struck up a conversation the previous day sat down on the bench next to him, uninvited, but not fearing to be turned away with a cutting word. That was his trouble, Carey reflected ruefully—children, domestic animals, and girls of the lower orders always seemed to be attracted to him, but he could not hold the notice, much less the affection, of someone so superior as Elena Melville. He felt very low.

"La, sir," Mary was saying, "you do talk lovely. Most gen'lemen wouldn't look twice at a poor flower girl, never mind remember 'er name and talk to 'er like she was a friend of 'is."

Carey had to smile at that. "Somehow, Mary, I cannot believe that you lack gentlemen admirers."

"Oh, well," Mary replied saucily, tossing her head, "admirers is one thing and gen'lemen another, ain't it? A clever girl can always find an admirer, but who needs 'em, I say."

When Carey immediately lapsed into gloom again, she said, "There was a nob what lived on this street not so long ago, me dad told me—number sixty-two. A royal duke, 'e was. Would you be acquainted with him, sir?"

"At the risk of lowering myself in your esteem, Mary, I must confess I don't know any royal dukes."

"Oh, well, I don't suppose you'd want to know this

one—not that he was a bad sort exactly. Very fat and jolly, 'e was. Bought flowers from me dad for 'is lady, though I 'ear they wasn't married. I even saw him once or twice meself as a kid. 'E had ever so many fine carriages and 'orses. Mrs. Clarke, 'is lady's name was, now I remember it."

"Good heavens, you don't mean the Duke of York?" Carey exclaimed, interested despite his preoccupation.

"Aye, that's the one." She looked at him hopefully. "You sure you don't know 'im?"

"Every man in the army knew the commander-in-chief—by reputation." Carey laughed. "And Mrs. Clarke, too. What a bumblebroth that was!"

For a few minutes, Carey managed to forget his own troubles in telling a fascinated Mary the story of the disgrace Mary Anne Clarke had brought upon her lover, Frederick, Duke of York, the Regent's younger brother, by selling army commissions behind his back.

Presently, however, Mary sighed and said she must go back to work before her dad caught her diddle-daddling.

"'Ere, sir," she said, rising from the bench, "'ow about a bunch of violets for yer lady—or mayhap a few rosebuds in silver paper. Nothing like flowers to turn a lady sweet."

Carey contemplated the posies Mary held out to him, then looked at the basket on her arm. He was visited with a momentary suspicion that her father had sent her to find him with a full basket and the express purpose of soft-talking him into buying something. Well, he had nothing to lose. He reached into his pocket.

"How much for the lot?"

Mary's face lit up. "The whole basket?"

"That's right. How much?"

"Er . . . half a crown, sir?"

Carey handed her two florins. "Here you are then, and something to buy your dad a tot after work."

"Oh, sir!" said Mary, blushing. She promptly concealed the coins in her apron and, with a little curtsey, handed him the basket. "Thank you, sir."

"Now here is what you must do for me in return . . ."

*   *   *

It was a small start, but Carey felt better as soon as he had dispatched Mary to deliver her basket of flowers to Elena's door, along with a note that said simply, "I love you."

Tomorrow he would send her another small gift—he did not want her returning his offerings on the excuse that they were too costly for her to accept—with the same message. He would not call on her again, only to be turned away, but he would not let her put him out of her mind, either. Sooner or later, she would have to see him, if only to beg him to stop.

It was a humbling plan, but he did not care a fig about that, so long as it brought him a word with Elena.

He was delighted when it took only a lace handkerchief, a bottle of Hungary water, and a tin of Chinese tea—all delivered by Mary in a basket of flowers—to bring her out of hiding three days later.

He was again chatting amiably with Mary on the bench in the square when he became aware of the gate creaking open. He looked up and saw Elena standing a mere six feet away. She looked the picture of a classical Greek maiden, but she was dressed in a very English rose-striped day dress and a green bonnet with artificial roses on it. Carey gazed at her in rapturous admiration, unable to locate his tongue. Mary obligingly scurried around Elena and out of the square, closing the gate carefully behind her.

"Dearest!" Recovering his speech, Carey rose and went to his beloved, taking her gloved hands in his. She lowered her eyes, but did not attempt to pull her hands out of his grip. He looked at her more closely and saw that her only color was in her dress and the flowers in her bonnet.

"My dear, you are looking quite pale. Have you been ill? I'm so sorry . . . had I known . . ."

She gave a watery little chuckle. "Doubtless you would have sent more flowers. The house already looks like a country fete."

He smiled and squeezed her hands more tightly. It was

all he could do not to kiss her there and then, for all the world to see, but he confined his ardor to his intense gaze. Elena ventured to raise her eyes to meet it, then lowered them again in confusion. It was not like Elena to show uncertainty, Carey thought, wondering again if she was ill.

"Tell me what the matter is, dearest."

"Please, Carey, I only came to say you must stop this nonsense of sending gifts and hanging about my doorstep. It is very charming of you to be so . . . so persistent, but it will not serve."

"It served to bring you here."

"But this must be the last time. I have said good-bye, and I meant it."

"But you have not said why. Do you not think you owe me some explanation? Has it something to do with your family—your brother? Does he disapprove of me?"

Elena started, and her face turned even paler. Carey grasped her elbow as she sank onto the bench. He sat beside her, moving close, both to keep their conversation private and simply to be as near to her as possible.

"It *is* your brother! But he is not your legal guardian, and Melville approves of me. What possible objection could—"

"No, no, it is not that!" Elena fluttered her hands despairingly and took a deep breath before continuing. "That is, not entirely. But he—my family—has led me to the conclusion that there is too great a difference between our cultures and our stations . . . Mr. Fairfax . . . to ensure a successful union between us. There would always be misunderstandings, differences we could not reconcile . . ."

"But that is nonsense! And for heaven's sake, don't call me Mr. Fairfax, as if we'd just been introduced!" Carey said, failing to keep a peevish tone out of his voice. "There is nothing we cannot reach an understanding about—if only to disagree—if we but talk about it."

"I cannot!" Elena said, her voice catching on a sob. She made a movement to rise, and Carey caught her arm. She pulled at it, but he would not yield. She sat down again.

Carey, seeing her lose her habitual calm for the first time, responded by taking it on himself. He made soothing noises in a low voice, then pulled a handkerchief out of his pocket and handed it to her. She sniffed into it.

"Never mind, dearest," he said gently. "I will not press you. One day all this will come clear, and it will no longer matter—if only you do not send me away."

"That day may never come. I cannot ask you to wait. You must not be seen to—that is, you must not be associated with me in any way."

Carey resisted the strong impulse to demand an explanation of this extraordinary statement and instead changed the subject. Perhaps there was another way to wear down stone.

"I can wait. I already have enough memories of you to sustain my patience for a long time."

He ventured to stroke her cheek and went on, "Do you remember when we went walking in the garden at Wyckham and you admired the roses? Bascomb was so taken with you that he immediately decided to name one of the new roses he had developed after you. So you see, you will always live at Wyckham in one way. And I will never give up hope that you will live there in all ways one day."

When Elena said nothing more, he leaned closer to whisper in her ear. All the fond dreams of installing Elena as the mistress of his home and seeing her raise their children in the peaceful setting of the country where Wyckham stood came out in words more eloquent than he had believed himself capable of. It was true that of late he had allowed these dreams to take vivid form in his mind as an antidote to the unthinkable possibility of Elena's never setting foot in his gardens again, and this no doubt lent immediacy to his descriptions.

" . . . I will never forget those days, particularly not the day when you said that you wished you had had such a place to live in when you were a child, and that you could think of no greater happiness than to see your own children—"

"No!" She stood up so abruptly this time that Carey was unable to stop her. "No!" she repeated, "you must stop remembering—stop hoping. You must find someone else to fulfill your dreams, Carey, for I cannot. Please do not continue to torture me so!"

With that, she picked up her skirts and ran toward the gate, jerking it open just as he caught up with her. She pulled away and ran into the street, where a shout brought her to an abrupt halt.

"'Ere, missus! Watch where yer goin', can't you!"

The hackney driver, busily bringing his plunging horses under control, was further able only to hurl a few breathless curses down at the foolish woman who had run into the street without looking where she was going. But when an equally heedless young man followed her, his curses rained down more loudly and fluently, finally catching the distracted gentleman's attention.

Carey glanced up, muttered "Beg your pardon!" and took the horse's bridle in his fist. He spoke quietly into the animal's twitching ear for a moment, which served finally to calm him, but by that time, Elena was out of sight.

The hack went on its way, and Carey sighed. It was apparent that Elena would tell him no more than she had, which was little enough, while she was in this mysterious state of agitation. It was equally apparent that if he continued on his present course, he would only place her in danger in ways he could not anticipate, not the least of which was an accident in the street. He would have to wait and watch for an opportunity to approach her in some other way. He could only hope his patience would serve him until then.

He hailed the next hack and directed the driver to deliver him to his club—and the soothing company of whichever of his former army comrades were on the premises and whatever form of liquid anesthesia might be on hand to drown his troubles, at least for today.

Tomorrow he would consult his brother-in-law. Yes, that was what he would do. Duncan might not have an answer, but he would not take Carey's troubles lightly either. He never did when it really mattered.

Chapter 10

~

Sleep had eluded Lady Kedrington, and she awoke before dawn, her mind still turning over the questions she had been pondering the night before. Her husband had not come home before she went to bed, where she had slept only fitfully without the security of his presence in the next room.

Further thought had divided her mind about his mysterious activities—whatever they might prove to be. She had long thought that he had too little to do when they came to town and only came because she enjoyed it and it did give him a chance to meet people who lived too far from their country estate to visit regularly. She knew he occasionally conducted estate business from Brook Street, but it could not be sufficient to occupy his active mind for long. Therefore, whatever he was up to with Robin Campbell had to be a good thing.

On the other hand, she could not shake a sense of there being some danger involved in the undertaking. He was well able to take care of himself, of course, and she did not think he would take foolish risks. Yet she could not help worrying.

When, therefore, she heard the creak of a floorboard in the adjoining room, she immediately rose and knocked on the door of her husband's dressing room.

"Psst! Duncan, are you awake?"

Without waiting for an answer, she opened the door,

only to be brought up short by the sight of her husband nearly fully dressed. Indeed, by the light of the single candle he had lit, she saw that he was in the processing of undressing for bed, not dressing for the day.

"I *knew* it has been too quiet in here all night, even for you," she declared. "Wherever have you been?"

"Not with you, I regret to say," he replied with a sigh in his voice. "But if you will be patient a moment longer, I shall join you and explain all."

Antonia accepted this, although not without muttering under her breath as she returned to her bedroom about the patience she had been forced to show of late and whenever did Duncan explain all of anything.

Nonetheless, by the time she had climbed up into her bed again, puffed up the pillows behind her back so that she could sit up, and run her fingers lightly through her hair in a belated attempt to make some order of it, the viscount had entered her room in his small clothes and climbed in beside her.

He leaned over to kiss her and murmured, "You always smell so delicious after you have been sleeping."

Antonia would never have revealed that she secretly perfumed her pillowslips every night even had she thought to say so. Instead, she allowed herself to relax into her husband's embrace and enjoy his slow, sweet kiss. However, when she felt herself sliding blissfully back into a supine position under the weight of his insistent body, she pulled herself up again, shook her bemused mind clear, and said, a little breathlessly, "Oh, no. Explain first!"

"Explain what?" he murmured, burying his mouth in the hair behind her ear. He knew very well that this was a particularly sensitive spot, and it was all she could do to push him away from it and slap his wandering hands away from her neckline.

"Duncan! You were going to tell me where you have been."

He raised his head, looked into her frowning face, and sighed again. "Robin Campbell asked me for my advice."

"Oh, yes—the mysterious summons. What sort of odd thing did you discover was going on?"

He pushed himself up into a sitting position and resigned himself to answering her questions.

"If you read Robin's letter, why are you interrogating me?"

"It wasn't a letter. It was barely a note, and even more terse than you are about explanations."

He searched her expression again. "If I tell you, you must promise not to reveal it to another soul."

"Duncan! Have I ever repeated anything you tell me in confidence?"

"Well, no. But I had to say that, since it concerns other people, not just ourselves."

"I promise. Now what is it?"

He gave her a brief summary of the events of the past two nights, beginning with Robin Campbell's original concern about the authenticity of one panel of one of the friezes. Antonia's eyes lit with excitement.

"But how thrilling! Who do you suppose could have stolen it? And why?"

"How would be more to the point. If we discovered that, we could guess the who easily enough. At the moment, however—and this may be only my late lack of sleep speaking—I am inclined to think there was never a theft at all and the fake piece was always there. There may have been an exchange for heaven only knows what reason during their troubled transit to England. The piece may have been put up to replace a damaged panel when the wall was still in place, goodness knows how long ago."

He pulled a pillow out from behind his wife, who was now sitting up without the aid of any support, and lay down with his head on it.

"And furthermore," he said, "I don't care. I'm getting too old for midnight sentry duty."

"Oh, pooh, you're just getting soft. I've spoiled you, that's what it is."

"In that case, you won't mind indulging me a little longer and letting me get some sleep."

Antonia thought for a moment, began "But Duncan . . . ," and looked down at her husband. He was fast asleep. He had not yet, it seemed, lost his ability to fall asleep quickly and at any time that he needed to do so. She supposed he would be awake and himself again in no more than three or four hours, so she resolved to consider the problem herself in the meanwhile.

She slid quietly out of bed again, went through the viscount's dressing room into his bedroom, and pulled the bell there. Milford would respond, and since he was not unaccustomed to finding his master and mistress in each other's bedrooms at unusual hours, he would not object to bringing her a cup of coffee . . . and perhaps a roll and a pot of jam . . . and cream . . .

Three hours later, Antonia's fourth cup of coffee was cooling unattended on the breakfast room table while she perused the morning papers. That she was looking for something specific was evidenced by the discarded pages on the floor and the fact that she had broached the *Times* before Kedrington had a chance to read it.

She was reading a particularly interesting item in this chronicle, in fact, when the viscount, looking as refreshed as if he had just spent a week in hibernation in the country, entered the room.

"Is that my newspaper you are clutching? If you wrinkle the foreign news, I warn you, I shall claim it as grounds for divorce."

Disregarding this threat, she said, "I have just been reading a most interesting piece about Sir John Drummond. Did you know that he has spoken in the House about the disadvantages of displaying the marbles in that building Robin is guarding? He demands that more stringent security measures be taken."

"I was aware of something of the kind."

"Well, of course you were. But does it not strike you as suspicious?"

Kedrington sat down with a plateful of eggs and bacon, but stayed his fork to glance at his wife.

"I fail to see why. He believes the hall to be unsafe and unworthy of the high order of art displayed in it—or the other way around, I don't recall at the moment. I daresay someone will have pointed out to him by now that mold is scarcely a threat to centuries-old marble and that if the building fell in on them, they would only get dusty. It is Robin and his fellows who would suffer in the event of such a catastrophe."

"But that is precisely it, don't you see?"

"No."

"You know that anything Sir John says in public is only a mask for his private activities."

"And . . .?" Kedrington inquired over a mouthful of egg.

"He must therefore believe that there is some danger to the marbles. If they were stolen, he would be credited with foresight and good sense, not to mention that he would score a moral victory against poor Lord Elgin."

"*Poor* Lord Elgin?"

"I only meant he is no match for someone as devious as Sir John. You know I have little patience for weaklings, and my feeling sorry for them does not mean I feel obliged to *like* them."

"Disregarding your unjust assessment of Elgin, my love, that is a distinction I have never known you to make before. Indeed, I recall a certain scullery maid who would have stolen us blind because you felt sorry for her and insisted we keep her on even after she was caught with your silver earbobs in her pocket."

"Well, I could not let her go to prison for the rest of her life for a momentary lapse! Those earbobs were not even particular favorites of mine—they were my sister-in-law's discards, as I recall. But we are getting away from the point, Duncan."

"I beg your pardon. What *is* the point?"

"That Sir John Drummond is perfectly capable of arranging for the theft of one or more of the marbles in order to further his political career."

Antonia leaned forward, prepared to offer a spirited defense of her theory, but found her husband temporarily speechless. Indeed, he was gazing out the window and seemed to be giving the idea serious consideration.

"Much as I dislike encouraging your fancies," he said at last, "I must confess that I do not find this one entirely outside the realm of possibility."

"Can I take that to mean you will investigate it?"

He gave her a sharp look. "Is that what you intended when you fabricated it?"

"I did not fabricate it! Here"—she handed him the newspaper—"see for yourself."

He took the *Times* and folded it neatly before placing it out of Antonia's reach.

"And what will *you* be investigating the meanwhile?"

"I declare, Duncan, sometimes you frighten me. Can you read everyone's mind so readily?"

He smiled. "Only yours, my dear, and then only through years of studying and admiring it."

She got up, went around to his side of the table, and kissed him soundly. Then she patted his mouth with her linen napkin, observed that he tasted like nutmeg, and sat down again, having thoroughly silenced him so that she could speak at least three sentences without interruption.

"I shall meanwhile learn all I can about this mysterious brother of Elena's."

This unexpected revelation further astonished his lordship, who sat back in his chair and regarded his wife with renewed admiration.

"I did not know she had a brother."

"Nor did anyone else. That is the mystery. Furthermore, he is Greek."

"Not a mystery. So is Elena."

"A Greek *nationalist*."

"Ah. I begin to see your drift."

"I told you I am not so illogical as you think."

"Do you have any reason to suspect this young man's involvement with the stolen—presumably stolen—panel?"

"No, but one supposes his movements can be traced."

"If he is found to exist in the first place."

"Oh, I do not doubt that. Arthur Melville told us all about him—at least, so far as he *knew* anything about him. What is more, I believe that Dimitri's existence—or more to the point, his activities—may be the reason behind Elena's breaking it off with Carey."

"Did Carey know she had a brother?"

"No, it was as much a surprise to him as to me, which is in part why I believe Dimitri had a part in her decision—much against her will, I am convinced, even if Carey is not—to call off the engagement."

During this fervent speech, Kedrington pulled out his pocket notebook. "What did you say was the brother's name?"

"Dimitri Metaxis. You were going to investigate Sir John's activities."

"So I shall. And I shall inform you of my findings, as I expect you will do as well."

Antonia smiled. "All will be revealed tonight."

"That will be fast work. Nonetheless, I shall be home early—in anticipation."

"You do not intend to spend the night with a collection of cold Greeks again, then?"

He put away his notebook, rose, and leaned over to kiss her before setting out on his mission.

"I had much rather spend it with a warm wife."

"I shall endeavor to please."

"You always do, my love."

When Kedrington had gone out, Antonia sighed and rose to dress for her own morning activities. She congratulated herself for not adjuring Duncan to be careful, for he would only tell her not to worry. She would worry whether he said it or not, so she consoled herself as best she could with her restraint.

"I know he dislikes being fussed over," she said later to Julia Wilmot, referring to her concern that Kedrington found little to amuse himself in town, "even if he never says anything to that effect."

"He has always been so," Julia confirmed. Antonia had walked to Berkeley Square, accompanied by one of her footmen, and now sat in the aunts' parlor, bringing them up to date on the news from Brook Street. She had been vaguely disappointed to find Hester at home as well as Julia, for she dared not reveal any details about Kedrington's nocturnal activities in front of her. Hester never intended to repeat anything she heard in confidence, but she had been known to do so inadvertently on more than one occasion, and Julia's scolding had done nothing to break her of this unfortunate tendency.

"Indeed, yes," Hester now chimed in. "Why, I recall that he broke his arm when he was a boy and made so light of it that we nearly did not discover that the limb was broken in time to have it set."

Antonia smiled at Hester, prepared to listen to a story she had heard several times before, to make up for her unkind, if unspoken, thoughts about Miss Coverley.

"Of course, he comes to town to see us," Julia said, having neither reason nor desire to encourage Hester. "Or at least in part to do so," she conceded. "Even I am not so vain as to suppose he does it solely for our sake."

"And he is most conscientious of his duty in writing to us regularly when he is residing in Leicestershire," Hester confirmed. "As you do, Antonia, dear," she added thoughtfully.

"Speaking of duty," Julia said, "is the match between Carey and Miss Melville definitely off?"

"Oh, no!" Antonia exclaimed. "At least—I do not believe so. I know that Carey's feelings have not changed, and I believe that Elena's have not either. I have every hope of a happy ending still."

"You were always romantical," Julia remarked, as if commenting on her being too short for beauty or afflicted with a poor singing voice.

Antonia had long ceased taking umbrage at any fault Julia might perceive in her, but before she could explain her reasons for thinking so, Hester asked, "Have you spoken with Miss Melville, then?"

"I'm afraid not—only with her guardian. But he told us something that leads me to believe that Elena broke off the engagement for reasons other than that her feelings had changed."

Both ladies looked expectant, and Antonia related the story of the mysterious brother and her suspicions that he had something to do with the matter.

"And what does the brother say?" Julia asked.

"That's just it, you see. No one has seen him—except, presumably, Elena. Mr. Melville has not, and Carey did not know anything about him."

"Miss Melville did not tell him she has a brother?" Julia said. "That seems very odd to me." ·

It seemed very odd to Antonia also, but she would not even imply a criticism of Elena in front of Julia Wilmot. "I expect her estrangement with her family is something Elena regrets, and she was therefore reluctant to mention it. I'm sure she would have done . . . eventually."

"Perhaps he is the black sheep of the family," Hester suggested, her eyes lighting at the possibility of such a drama among people she knew, who were generally very proper and uninteresting. "Has he been cast out of the family bosom? Has he done something dreadful to bring disgrace on them?"

Julia sniffed disapprovingly, but Antonia smiled. "Much as I would like to provide you with an exciting *on-dit*, Hester, dear, I fear the estrangement will turn out to be the result of some silly misunderstanding, nothing more. Still," she went on, "I wish I knew how to find Dimitri and confront . . . that is, speak to him about it and hear his side."

Hester leaned forward, still hopeful. "Dimitri? What an exotic name! But of course, he is Greek, is he not?"

"Yes. Dimitri Metaxis."

Antonia glanced hopefully at Julia, who was gazing pensively into her cup of camomile tea. Hester's interest was gratifying, and she had a wide circle of friends among whom she would now doubtless inquire about Dimitri, but it was Julia's help she wanted most. Antonia suspected that Julia had never entirely approved of Carey's engagement to Elena Melville, particularly since she had had no hand in bringing the match about, but Julia was not so devoted to the sanctity of the Heywood line and the respectability of anyone connected with it that she would object to a love match or do anything to prevent it.

"Perhaps I may make a few inquiries," she said at last.

Antonia let out her breath and said, "Oh, thank you, Aunt Julia. I hoped you would say that."

Julia glared at her. "Nonsense. You came here planning to cajole me into helping you. I know your ways, young woman!"

"Yes, Aunt," Antonia conceded meekly.

"Oh, how thrilling!" Hester said. "A mystery to be solved!" She immediately rose and said she was going out now to begin making inquiries of her own, and would Antonia care to join her?

Antonia declined the invitation, and when Hester had closed the door behind her, she remained seated opposite Julia.

"That is the first time in my memory that I have agreed to do something for someone without first hearing the entire story."

"Why, Aunt Julia," Antonia said, pretending surprise, "what can I have left out?"

"A great deal, I suspect. Now tell me."

"Yes, Aunt Julia."

Chapter 11

Lord and Lady Kedrington quite forgot the important matters they had intended to discuss that night, for after an excellent supper, washed down with a considerable quantity of champagne, those matters seemed not at all important. What they talked of by the light of the single candle in her ladyship's bedroom was only of themselves, and when their voices fell silent and the candle guttered out, their thoughts were only for each other and the pleasures each found in the other's company.

The following morning, however, as Antonia sat up in bed, waiting for rolls and coffee to be sent up to her and perusing the last quarter's *Edinburgh Review* in lieu, temporarily, of more recent news, she recalled something she had meant to ask her husband that had nothing to do with their conversation the night before—or its lack in the small hours.

His lordship was in his dressing room being shaved, so she was obliged to call loudly, "Dearest, have you ever considered going back to the sort of work you did in Spain—you know, for the Duke?"

"If you mean spying," he replied, "you can say the word in Milford's presence. He was there too."

"I beg your pardon, Milford"—a polite murmur of acknowledgment emerged from his lordship's valet—"but, Duncan, have you?"

"Certainly not. First, we are no longer at war. Second,

we are not in Spain. And third, I don't have the time, what with managing Windeshiem so that it produces a sufficient income for you to live in the style to which I have accustomed you."

"Oh, pooh. I am not *that* extravagant. Come in here and help me finish this champagne. Perhaps that will change your mind."

He came into her room then, rubbing his chin, and closed the dressing room door behind him, shutting out the sounds of shaving basin and water being removed from the vicinity. He sat down on the bed and kissed Antonia's cheek.

"Oh, you do smell delightful when you've just shaved—and you don't scratch when you kiss."

She returned the kiss, and for several moments forgot her train of thought.

"But if you were to, say—"

"No," he said.

"How do you know what I was about to say?"

There was a decided gleam in his eye as he said, "It doubtless had something to do with changing my habits, but I am too far along in my dotage to do that."

He took the *Edinburgh* out of her hand and laid it on the table on his side of the bed. "Anyway, it's my guess that Miss Melville's brother threatened her with something if she goes on seeing Carey."

That effectively diverted her. "What? Oh, do you think so? But why?"

"Why do I think so? Because I discovered yesterday that young Dimitri has been running with a very shady crowd."

"I meant, why would he threaten her? And how did you find out who he's been keeping company with?"

"When you become ungrammatical, my love, I know you're thinking hard. But it's not so complicated. I know a few people in the foreign office who are intimately involved with the Elgin controversy, and they have been watching closely those patriots who want the marbles returned to Greece. Young Mr. Metaxis is one of them, yet there is no evidence that he has done anything but talk—and keep company with ruffians."

"But why has no one seen him, apart, presumably, from his sister?"

"No one particularly cares. Among our circle, no one is aware of his existence. Of the authorities monitoring the situation, no one has any reason to watch him more closely than anyone else. They know where he lives, but they could not tell me anything officially."

He paused and picked up a glass from the bedside table. "This is flat," he said, tasting the golden liquid in it.

"There's an unopened bottle on the dresser."

He eyed the bottle consideringly and finally said, "I think not. I have several errands to run today, and I do not care to be seen weaving about the streets."

"Where are you going?" she said, brushing an imaginary speck of dust from his collar. She was reluctant to see him go. "Will you see Carey?"

"I had not planned to do so, but I may well encounter him somewhere in my wanderings. Shall I give him a message for you?"

He looked at her and smiled, and she had the distinct impression that he was holding something back. She was certain that he did know where Dimitri Metaxis lived, but would not tell her. She also suspected that he knew more about the Greek patriot organization than he let on.

"You *are* going to nose about for clues!" she accused him.

He looked appalled. "My dear Lady Kedrington, wherever do you pick up such slang expressions?"

"At Wyckham, I daresay. Carey's hounds are forever 'nosing about' where they should not—and they stir up hornets' nests and annoy hedgehogs often enough to teach them a lesson that they never seem to learn."

"I shall take care where I put my nose," he said, interpreting her anecdote as a warning to be cautious. He rose from the bed, but she pulled on his hand.

"Dearest, if you do see Carey . . ."

He sat down again. "What?"

"You know I am as curious as you about Dimitri Metaxis and his intentions, but I am much more concerned for my brother's happiness. I will try again to call on Elena, but if I cannot reassure her that whatever difficulties have caused her to break off their engagement are not long-lasting, will you please speak to Carey?"

"What can I say?"

"The same thing—that everything will resolve itself somehow. He looks up to you, Duncan—he will believe you. If you are able, also, find him something to occupy his mind until this business is resolved."

"I do believe I am becoming quite talented in that particular skill."

"What do you mean?"

He leaned over to give her a good-bye kiss. "Only that I can lie with conviction—like a good spy."

"You are absurd. Give my love to Robin Campbell."

"Your love?"

"I do have a little left over, I think."

"Oh, in that case—" He came back to the bed and pulled up the covers as if he would get in, fully clothed, but Antonia laughed and pulled the sheets more firmly around her.

"Get away and go to your spying."

He got up. "Yes, your ladyship."

"And find out what is delaying my breakfast," she flung after him. "I'm famished!"

He went out, chuckling, and Antonia recalled, ruefully, how worried she had been he had nothing to do. Apparently, he had found more than enough to worry her for other reasons.

Lord Kedrington did make several calls in the vicinity of St. James's before signaling a hack to take him to Burlington House. His efforts to learn whether Sir John Drummond had an undisclosed purpose for his recent speech had thus far been fruitless, so he was glad that his wife had failed to ask him about that particular matter.

He smiled at himself. He still behaved like a smitten suitor, wanting Antonia to believe him invincible and all-powerful. It was not that she was unaware of his weaknesses—indeed, she had pointed them out unmercifully in the early days of their courtship—but she had not mentioned them, or not often, since their marriage, and he liked to hope that she no longer cared about them. He hoped even more fervently that she never had occasion to recall them.

His cab was just turning down Jermyn Street to bypass the traffic on Piccadilly when Kedrington spotted Carey Fairfax emerging from his club. By his disheveled look and uncertain gait, Kedrington guessed that his brother-in-law had spent the night there, and not in any lofty pursuit. He called up to the driver to pull over to the curb.

Carey squinted at the cab, as though wondering if he had called it, then groaned when he saw the face in the window and covered his eyes with his hand.

"Oh, Lord—Duncan! Just leave me to die in peace, can't you."

"Nonsense, you can't do it on a public street. Your sister would never speak to you again. Get in."

Still grumbling, Carey stumbled into the cab and fell back against the seat. "If I were dead, she couldn't talk to me anyway," he caviled.

"I'm glad to see that your mind has not entirely turned to liquid. But she wouldn't speak to me, either, and that fate I do not care to contemplate. What has Miss Melville said to you to cast you down so far into the depths?"

Evincing no surprise at Kedrington's perception, Carey poured out the entire tale of his last meeting with his beloved, not leaving out his haunting of her door, nor Mary, nor his nearly causing Elena to be run down in the street. Kedrington did not interrupt, but even so, by the time Carey finished this rotomontade, they had been waiting in the cab in front of Burlington House for several minutes.

Carey sighed, leaned back in his seat, and closed his eyes.

"You can't sleep here," Kedrington told him. "It isn't a hotel. Do you wish to keep the cab, or will you come inside with me? You can nap there, if you like, while I speak with Robin Campbell."

Carey opened one eye, faintly interested. "May as well come in," he mumbled. "Nothing better to do."

Shortly thereafter, Kedrington found himself studying the marbles as if he had not seen them a dozen times before. Robin Campbell had been escorting a party of scholars around the collection when they came in, and so they were obliged to wait for his attention.

"Don't see what the fuss is all about," Carey remarked, scowling back at a belligerent centaur. "What did you say this is supposed to represent?"

His brother-in-law regarded him balefully. "Has none of this been explained to you? Or were you just too besotted with Miss Melville's earlobe to pay attention when we were last here?"

Carey winced. "A low blow, your lordship. Don't Jackson teach you not to fight dirty?"

"He does, but I never followed that advice. Something's needed to knock sense into you."

Carey looked uncertain whether to challenge Kedrington or throw himself on his mercy and guidance. Robin Campbell joined them just at that moment, however, allowing Carey, after a perfunctory greeting, to sink back into the shadows and lick his wounds.

"What's the matter with him?" Robin asked, sotto voce, as they strolled along together ahead of Carey.

"Woman trouble."

"Not with the fair Elena? She seemed quite taken with him, which I admit struck me as odd, but there's no knowing what some girls fancy." Mr. Campbell had known Mr. Fairfax during their mutual military past and felt no qualms about abusing him to another friend.

Kedrington grinned, but then sobered quickly. "So I would have said to him only a short time ago, but he's beyond taking a joke just now. She broke it off with him, and he hasn't quite recovered."

"But why?"

Kedrington shrugged. "There's some mystery about that. My wife is on a crusade to uncover it, and I am charged in the meanwhile with keeping an eye on the rejected swain and finding him something to do to take his mind off his misery, so I brought him along with me today." He glanced back, but found Mr. Fairfax still following, hands in pockets and stopping occasionally to peer at a sculpture as if determined to become acquainted with it, however dull it might prove.

"I was surprised when he agreed to come in here with me," Kedrington continued, "but I suppose we may take it as a good sign—even if he has learned nothing about the marbles since he was first introduced to them."

"Have you?"

"Not directly. I apologize for not joining you last night, by the way, but I was . . . distracted."

"Please say no more. I scarcely expected you to spend every night here. Indeed, I am beginning to think I was needlessly alarmed and that you were right about the fake panel being part of the collection all along."

"That is what I thought when I left here the other morning."

Robin gave him a sharp look. "But you no longer think so? What has happened?"

"That is for you, perhaps, to tell me. Do you recall mentioning seeing a young man here who came several times?"

"Yes, I believe so. Why?"

"What did he look like?"

Robin thought about it for a moment, then said, "Dark, average height and weight. Good-looking. Possibly not English, although he dressed like an Englishman."

Kedrington nodded, satisfied. "I think that may have been Miss Melville's brother, a Greek patriot. You have not seen him since?"

"No, I am quite sure he has not been here. Her brother, you say? Do you suspect him of something?"

"I have no evidence to go on, but he is the most likely suspect to come along so far. He has been behaving in a secretive manner, but of course that may be for another reason entirely."

"Or it may be designed to distract us from other suspects. Looking for other suspects, that is."

"A valid point. Let us look at that panel again, shall we?"

They made their way to the frieze with the questionable panel and looked at it, Robin frowning and Kedrington looking pensive.

"Observe the lighting," Kedrington suggested.

"It is the same as before—as we arranged it."

"Quite right. Now follow me."

The tap of Robin's cane on the floor became more pronounced as he became less conscious of it, his mind being occupied with the puzzle Kedrington was hinting at.

They stopped in front of a vividly rendered relief figure of a horseman, his arm raised as if to urge on his steed, or the men who followed him.

"And here?"

Robin glanced around at the candle sconces on the wall and floor, where they were artfully concealed behind miniature plaster Ionic columns.

"You're on to something . . . it's dimmer here than it was." He examined the candles behind the pillars and saw that every other one had been snuffed out.

"Our culprits apparently had the same idea we did about distracting the eye from a flaw," Kedrington said, moving on to the next figure. "Observe this chariot."

Robin leaned closer for a more careful inspection.

"Oh, God . . . another one."

"What do you two find so fascinating in these old stones?" Carey demanded just then. "I've been trying to catch your attention forever. Well, five minutes, anyway."

Robin straightened up, and both he and Kedrington turned to look at Carey as if he had just turned to stone himself. Then they looked at each other as if the same thought had occurred to both at the same time.

"What?" Carey demanded, with greater liveliness than he had displayed all day.

Kedrington put his arm around Carey's shoulder. "My boy, I think you can give us valuable assistance in a matter of some importance."

"Do follow me to my office, gentlemen," Robin bade them, then led the way.

Chapter 12

Lady Kedrington was returning home from a visit with Julia Wilmot—to which she had been suddenly summoned by that lady and which had proved most intriguing, if not quite enlightening—when she chanced to see Arthur Melville walking down Bond Street. She signaled her coachman to stop, and when he pulled up a short distance down the street, Antonia leaned out just as her quarry came alongside.

"Mr. Melville!"

He stopped, glanced up, and smiled. Doffing his hat, he said cordially, "Good afternoon, Lady Kedrington. What a pleasure to see you."

"I was thinking just the same, sir. May I offer you a lift to wherever you are going? Better still, if you have half an hour to spare, will you not come with me and have your tea at Brook Street today?"

Melville looked as if he were torn by conflicting obligations, but it was only a moment before he made up his mind.

"Thank you so much. I should be delighted to accept your kind invitation."

Once again Antonia thought that Arthur Melville trod a fine line between obsequiousness and insolence, but before she could have second thoughts about renewing this acquaintance, the groom had jumped down and opened the door. Mr. Melville climbed in and took the seat opposite her. Again he removed his hat, but he said nothing more, allowing Antonia to choose the course of the conversation. She dismissed her flutter of irritation. She was, after all, not inviting him for his charming presence, but to learn what more she could about his ward's behavior.

Nonetheless, she thought it might be prudent to delay questioning him on that head until she had him firmly seated in her parlor and, further, that a little interest in the man himself might well loosen his tongue when it came to more important—in Antonia's view—matters.

"I cannot suppose you were on your way to a modiste or a dressmaker," she said with the kind of coquettish smile that her husband would have recognized as designed to prise some indiscretion out of an unsuspecting male. "That is, of course, why we ladies visit Bond Street, but I cannot imagine you engaged in so frivolous a pursuit as shopping."

He answered in an appropriately light manner. At least, Antonia thought, he did not entirely lack a sense of humor.

"In a manner of speaking, I was . . . shopping, that is to say. As you may recall, I take an amateur interest in the fine arts, and I was on my way to visit a new gallery that I had heard boasted some very fine drawings."

"Oh, I'm so sorry. I've kept you from your mission."

"It is no matter. The gallery will be there tomorrow."

"But I will have my coachman return you to Bond Street after we have refreshed ourselves. I would not wish you to miss acquiring a particularly fine work of art to a rival for delaying a day."

"I daresay there is very little I miss that is worth the acquisition," he said confidently. Antonia was interested to note that there was no hint of boasting in his tone, only the certainty of a man who knew what he was doing. She was unsure whether to feel reassured or apprehensive about this. She must not underestimate the man.

When they arrived at Brook Street, she was glad to see that her staff took their cue from her behavior and treated Arthur Melville as graciously as any other guest. Indeed, when Antonia took Trotter aside to ask him to use the best china, Melville was treated to a display of courtesy and deference that bordered on the overwhelming. If she could not trick him into letting something slip in conversation, Antonia thought, she could appeal to his ambition.

"I am so sorry you have not been able to visit us here before today," she began, as she poured tea herself, waving Trotter aside. "Naturally, I would not have expected you to come to dinner alone after Miss Melville decided that night to break off her engagement to Carey. You were quite correct not to think of it."

"To be frank," he said, "I did not think of it only because I was concerned about Elena's feelings."

"Naturally." Antonia smiled sweetly at him, offering him a plate of bread and butter. He took a slice.

"Has she confided nothing to you about her reasons for her action?"

"I'm afraid not. I was hoping she would feel easier about doing so if I did not press her, but thus far that plan has borne no fruit."

Antonia took a sip of tea and considered her next tack.

"It is a pity," she said, "that we have not been able to do more for Miss Melville—that is, in the way of introducing her socially. I blame my brother for being so secretive about his feelings for her, but then, I daresay he was swept away by love. You know how young people are."

Melville said nothing for a moment. Antonia sipped her tea and wished there were some sweet cakes. She rang the little bell on the tray to call Trotter, who shortly appeared with another tray of delicacies.

"In the course of a long engagement," she went on when she had fortified herself with a slice of currant cake, "we should have been able to introduce her to our friends and perhaps even escort her to Almack's. I know she has been to Wyckham with Carey, but it would have been pleasant to have her to Windeshiem as well for a longer period so that she might become known in the neighborhood. I expect that sort of life would be more to her liking in the end, but still, young ladies must go through these little rituals, must they not? I did myself, although I confess I rebelled quite publicly at some of them. Indeed, I was considered quite the hoyden."

She paused, then smiled again, forcing him to murmur that he would not have believed it.

"That is why I am so happy that my brother has found such a sensible, pretty-behaved girl. I daresay you had a great deal to do with that, Mr. Melville."

"I like to think I set a good example," he conceded. "One does not wish to be too strict, so that a young girl cannot enjoy her season, but neither does it do to be too permissive."

Antonia nodded sagely, then asked, "I don't suppose Elena has been presented at court?" She was pleased to see that this query arrested Mr. Melville's teacup halfway to his lips.

He recovered quickly, however, and gave a little laugh. "Oh, no. Indeed, I have never looked so high for her. And I suspect that it is an honor Elena would feel beyond her imaginings."

"You may be right," Antonia replied, pretending to consider this carefully while she mentally chastised herself for leading Melville on. "Miss Melville is far too modest and retiring. I daresay she would find the prospect as daunting as . . . as being singled out to perform on the pianoforte before the Regent. Of course, she would be only one of many young ladies being presented, and contact with royal personages would be of the briefest . . . still, I wonder if I might suggest it to her?"

Antonia thought it unlikely that Elena would ever agree to a presentation, even if it were possible, and even if the Kedringtons might be allowed to sponsor her—although there was no point in letting Arthur Melville know how unlikely this was. In addition, despite her modesty, Elena had a firm mind once it was made up, and if she did not wish to be presented, she would not be presented.

"I would, naturally, leave the decision entirely to Elena," Melville said.

She had been correct in thinking that even a tentative offer would make a strong impression. Melville positively beamed. She had him in her hand now.

"It is a pity that Miss Melville has no family to see to such things," Antonia went on, then leaned a little closer to her guest in a confiding manner. "We do still think of ourselves as her family, despite this temporary setback in her relationship with my brother. Do you not agree that it must be temporary? I cannot think otherwise."

"I sincerely hope that is the case," Melville said, still smiling. Antonia pressed her advantage.

"If only we could locate her brother. He might be able to persuade her to look to her own happiness, even give his blessing to her marriage."

"Unfortunately, as I believe I mentioned at our last meeting, Elena has been estranged from her family for some time," Melville said, a little more cautiously. He was glancing meaningfully at the teapot, but Antonia withheld the offer of a second cup, as if quite forgetting her hostess's duties in the emotion of thought that struck her.

"But surely not from her brother!" she breathed. "Is he not her only really close family? And if he is in England also . . ."

"That is by no means certain. He does not maintain any contact with us—or not with me, in any case, and I do not think Elena would keep from me any correspondence she may have had."

"Are you acquainted with Dimitri at all?"

"Yes, indeed, although I have not seen him since . . ."

He paused, and Antonia did not fill the silence, hoping he would say where and when he had seen Dimitri Metaxis. But Melville was thoroughly on his guard now.

"We have not heard from or about him since before we engaged our current house for the season."

Antonia sighed inwardly, but smiled brightly at her guest and at last remembered to refill his cup. "Well, that is a pity. Still, perhaps my husband may be able to locate him . . ."

A flash of alarm crossed Melville's face. "Oh, my dear Lady Kedrington, please do not put him to the trouble! I'm certain I can—that is, allow me to make a few inquiries, even perhaps a discreet advertisement in the *Times* . . . if I am unsuccessful, perhaps then we may impose upon his lordship."

Antonia smiled even more brightly, not attempting to hide her glee, but hoping Melville would see it as gratitude for his offer.

"Won't you have another scone, my dear sir? And the gooseberry jam is made at our country estate. It is quite delicious, I assure you."

When Antonia closed the door on her guest half an hour later, she leaned back against it and sighed aloud.

"Is there anything I may get you, my lady?" Trotter enquired blandly. "A restorative of some kind perhaps?"

"Do not be impertinent, Trotter. There are occasionally reasons to flatter persons whom one would ordinarily not invite to tea."

"Yes, madam," Trotter said stonily. Their butler was no longer surprised at anyone whom her ladyship or the viscount might bring into the house, but he did not have to approve of them. He had his standards.

"Thank you, Trotter," Antonia said, recognizing that flattery would get her nowhere with him, but grateful nonetheless for his unquestioning—and often eerily perspicacious—devotion to her every whim.

She went up to her room, feeling suddenly in need of a nap before dinner. It had been too long since she had been obliged to exercise her mind in a conversation, and she was sadly out of trim. She must begin to invite more stimulating guests to her own parties, to make up for the insipid gatherings she was obliged to attend outside her home. She wished Julia Wilmot would come to her occasionally.

She had been preemptorily summoned by her husband's aunt earlier that day and dared not refuse the summons, being hopeful that Julia had learned something about the mysterious Dimitri Metaxis. When she arrived in Berkeley Square, Hester had been away from home, which was not unusual, but Julia had been bursting with news, which was. She rarely varied from her calm delivery of even the most startling gossip.

"It is not gossip, my dear Antonia," Julia had assured her, when Antonia had completed the ritual of kissing her on the cheek, admiring her new cap, remarking on what a fine day it was, and making herself as comfortable as possible in the not very comfortable chair Julia put her visitors in. "You know I do not put credence in mere rumor—not until I have had it confirmed from at least three sources."

"You are more reliable than any Fleet Street dispatch," Antonia said, smiling and folding her hands in her lap for lack of anywhere else to put them in her armless chair.

"Good gracious, I should hope so," Julia replied acerbically. "Even the *Times* does not have my sources of information."

"What have your sources revealed lately?"

"One moment, please," Julia said. "Tell me what Kedrington has been up to lately."

"Has he not been to call on you?" Antonia temporized. "I'm sure he intended to."

"Not for nearly a week," Julia said, "although he has apparently been visiting any number of strange venues in the meanwhile."

Antonia tried not to laugh, but she felt her mouth twitch. "Well, he does have any number of . . . er, interesting friends."

Julia harrumphed and glared at Antonia, who finally gave up and giggled. "Oh, very well—since you will doubtless hear about it from somewhere . . . I believe I told you that Duncan has been . . . ah, assisting an old army friend who is the caretaker of the Elgin marbles at Burlington House. Doubtless, some other former soldiers are also involved, and it would be those men he has been seen with."

"And what is he doing to assist this person?"

Antonia mentally debated whether to tell Julia as much

as she herself knew about the missing sculpture and finally decided that if she was her husband's principal confidant, Julia was the second, and, as Antonia often feared, probably the more discreet of them. She settled on giving her a sketchy outline of the events of recent days, concluding, rather cravenly, that Julia could ask Duncan for further details.

Julia apparently decided to accept Antonia's version of the story for the time being and did not press her, saying only that she would put her mind to the mystery. Antonia had the impression that she did so even as they spoke, although she did not immediately respond to her tale of intrigue.

Instead, she said, "Talking of Montagu House reminds me of the scandal of the first duchess—although since she was the duke's second wife, I am not absolutely sure that the appellation applies."

Antonia recognized this diversion for what it was—Julia was able to think while talking, and talked to keep her listeners from interrupting her train of thought. She obediently played her part by making no remark, but merely nodding to indicate that she was dutifully treading this by-path behind her hostess.

"The duke spent all his money on building his new house and then repaired his fortune by marrying, after his first wife died, the Duchess of Albemarle, who was very rich. She was also completely insane."

Antonia raised her eyebrows and looked interested.

"She declared that she would marry no one but a crowned head, so Montagu had to convince her that he was the emperor of China. She married him, but thereafter insisted that everyone who served her do so on bended knee."

Julia paused here, and Antonia looked expectant. Julia frowned off into space for a moment, and then asked offhandedly, "What is the name of Kedrington's friend—the one who is keeping guard at Burlington House?"

Not on bended knee, Antonia thought, but said promptly, "Robin Campbell. I suppose his first name must be Robert, but I know little about him other than that he is very personable and comes, I believe, from a Scottish family."

"You seem to know little about a great deal this morning," Julia remarked dryly.

Antonia judged it best not to respond to this gibe, and presently Julia asked, "And who does Kedrington believe to be behind this plot?"

"He has not formed any definite opinion on that head, since there are a number of possibilities." Antonia hoped that Julia would not ask her to enumerate these, but apparently Julia felt herself capable of thinking of them herself, for she did not ask.

Suddenly, however, she said, "Do you recall asking me about Dimitri Metaxis?"

At last! Antonia's ears warmed in anticipation. "Yes, indeed. Have you heard something, Aunt Julia?"

"Possibly no more than you have."

Antonia doubted this, but dutifully replied, "Well, I told you that he is Miss Melville's brother, and that I fear he had something to do with Elena's break with Carey. Other than that, I know only, from Elena's guardian, that he is an ardent Greek patriot—and even *that* is thus far an unsupported supposition."

"That appears to be true. I have also learned that he is an artist—even, I am assured, a talented one, if not brilliant. He has done numerous drawings of the Elgin marbles, which may be purchased at several galleries in town."

Antonia had not expected this, but was, when she thought about it, not surprised. Her next thought was a surprise, however.

"Why—that must be why Miss Melville was so taken aback when we saw the Drummonds' collection of drawings! She must have recognized them as her brother's work and . . ."

Julia regarded her quizzically. "And what?"

Antonia was uncertain. Why should Elena have been surprised to see them if she knew Dimitri had done them, or even if she had not known? The marbles would seem a natural subject for a young Greek artist proud of his heritage.

"Perhaps she did not know at the time that he was in town," she ventured.

"That would be my guess," Julia said. "Apparently he has been staying at Grillon's Hotel, but we could not find him in at any time."

"We? Surely, you did not go there yourself, Aunt Julia?"

"Certainly not. And you need not fear that I sent Hester. I am not so foolhardy. Webster went on a pretext that I will not reveal to you, but it has availed us nothing—except to put Webster in good odor with the manager of the hotel, so that if Mr. Metaxis does go to ground, we will know it, although his comings and goings are reportedly irregular, to say the least."

Antonia jumped up to hug Julia. "Dearest aunt, you are invaluable! I shall tell Duncan at once."

"You tell him I want to see him, nothing more," Julia instructed her. "When he deigns to call on me again, I shall tell him myself."

"That is coercion, you know."

"Yes, I do. But if it is the only way to get my nephew to do his duty by an old lady, I do not hesitate to employ it."

Antonia laughed and rose to take her leave, promising to deliver the message exactly.

"And see that you call back yourself soon," Julia shot after her as Antonia left, "and not only when you want something!"

Chapter 13

"Well, Robin," Kedrington said, "I am somewhat reluctant to leave you in the tender care of my wayward brother-in-law this evening, but I trust you can prevent his wandering the streets unsupervised."

"Unfair!" Mr. Fairfax protested, laughing. "I'm in fighting trim again and ready for any rumpus."

"That's what I'm afraid of."

Robin assured Kedrington that they would not be alone with the marbles that night in any case, whereupon Kedrington admitted that he had avenues of his own to pursue.

The three gentlemen were gathered in Campbell's office just before the display was to open to the day's visitors. Carey had spent the previous night there, but did indeed seem his usual self, despite lack of sleep. Kedrington envied him his youthful resilience.

"I've talked to Winslow," Robin said. "You haven't met him yet, but he's stopping at Hollister's place as well. He was with the engineers, and he's bringing some more of his old regiment tonight to patrol. They will also have a look at the marbles and perhaps suggest ways we have not thought of by which they might have been spirited out of here."

"I believe half the army must be living in that house with you," Kedrington remarked, "but I'm glad to hear you've enlisted some more useful assistance."

"Now just a minute—!" Carey interrupted. "I've hardly

had a chance to help, and you've already put me down as useless."

"I have done no such thing," Kedrington said mildly. "I concede that you have been called in somewhat belatedly. I was referring to myself, not being here when the second piece went missing."

"But you spotted it," Robin said. "I might not have done so."

"Let us not waste breath in reassuring ourselves that we are doing all we can, and simply do it."

Carey saluted. "Yes, sir, captain . . . er, major. What rank did you get discharged with anyway, Duncan?"

Kedrington grinned. "Officially, colonel—and officially, I still hold that rank, which is more than I can say for *you*, Lieutenant Fairfax."

"I suppose that means that you may *officially* pull rank."

"I never did so in Spain, and I have no intention of starting now. Lieutenant Campbell—"

"Sir!" Lieutenant Campbell snapped to attention.

"Don't you start. Just ask Winslow to have a look around and give me his impressions later. I shall return after dark."

"Don't Tonia ask where you go off to every night?" Carey inquired.

"Not every night," Kedrington replied, smiling. Carey's face turned pink, and Robin laughed.

"You'd better be off," he said to the viscount, "while he's speechless."

"That's more than I will be by tonight," Kedrington said. "I'm off to the House of Commons."

The ancient Royal Chapel of St. Stephen in the Palace of Westminster, in which the House of Commons met, was a cavernous building with stained-glass windows and high turrets at each corner, redolent of age, history, and dust. The speeches today were as dry as the air, and sparsely attended. Kedrington seated himself discreetly in the shadows of the visitors' gallery, observed that Sir John

Drummond was present, and made himself comfortable, prepared to wait.

Drummond left the chamber without speaking, however, and Kedrington rose to intercept him in the corridor.

"Ah, Kedrington," Drummond said, emerging from the chambers, his robe and wig left behind. "Come to take your place in the Lords at last, have you?"

Kedrington grinned. "And bore myself into an early grave? Certainly not."

"You could liven these ancient stones up with a few good speeches."

"I'm a man of few words, John."

Drummond eyed him skeptically. "I expect you've come to extract a few from me rather. What do you want, Duncan?"

"To take you to dinner at my club."

"In exchange for what?"

"My dear Drummond, how suspicious you are. I should like to hear what is happening in Parliament from a live source rather than the arid columns of the *Times*, nothing more. I assure you, I have no special agenda."

"So you say. I suspect you will get whatever it is out of me without my knowing I have given it away."

"If you have nothing to hide, my dear fellow, you have nothing to lose either. White's?"

Kedrington was a member of both Brooks's and White's clubs, since he was too discreet to reveal a partiality to either the Whigs or the Tories, and neither group wished to chance losing his support—should he ever reveal where it lay—by blackballing him from the center of their social universe. Drummond, on the other hand, was firmly in the Tory camp, and so it was to White's that the two gentlemen repaired.

"The old place isn't the same since George left," Kedrington observed when they had made themselves comfortable in a private parlor with a view of St. James's and broached a bottle of claret in anticipation of their meal.

"Which one?" Drummond said. "Byron's in Italy and

Brummell's somewhere in France, I imagine, living in the wretched circumstances so many debtors come to. Did you attend Christie's auction of his Chapel Street leavings?"

"Some of the leavings, as you call them, were very fine pieces, but no, I did not attend. I attempted to assist Brummell while he was still here, but by the time I came back to the country from Spain two years ago, he was already too far down the path to ruin to be turned back."

"You won't see anything you may have lent him again."

"I did not expect to. It was not a great amount. I referred previously to Byron, however."

"I recall now that you were friends," Drummond said, eyeing his companion consideringly. Their dinner was brought in just then, and after the rack of lamb had been served with a professional flourish and the waiter had departed, Drummond went on, "I also recall from our conversation the last time we met that you share our passionate poet's sentiments about the Parthenon marbles."

Kedrington smiled. "Who is quizzing whom here, John? I thought you expected me to attempt to oil Parliamentary secrets out of you."

"An anticipatory defensive thrust, my dear Duncan."

Kedrington's smile was less forced now. Drummond had drunk most of the claret and was already less able to defend himself than he thought. He set about to enjoy his roast lamb.

Both gentlemen concentrated on their food with a minimum of conversation until the table was cleared and cheese and port were introduced. Drummond took a generous swallow of the wine, remarked on the fine quality of the club's cellars, and said, "I suppose you want to know what's been said in the House lately about the marbles."

"I know what's been said in public," Kedrington said, carefully paring an Edam cheese. "I wonder what's been discussed behind closed doors."

Drummond shrugged. "The deed being done, no one cares to worry the subject any longer—save those friends of Elgin's who are fighting a rear-guard action for his rights."

"He is to be a trustee of the museum, is he not?"

"A mere sinecure. There is no money attached to it to relieve his debts. His friends are looking to secure him some kind of pension for his foreign service, since the fruits of his travels have netted him so little."

"But nothing has been said about the marbles themselves?"

"I doubt half the members have seen them. Artistic sensitivity is not an outstanding characteristic of the nobility of England."

"You have it."

Drummond smiled. "Perhaps, but I am the first to admit I am most interested in works that have high intrinsic value as well. Their subject matter, and particularly their symbolic value, mean little to me unless I can get a good price for them at auction."

Kedrington studied his companion, wondering if he was perhaps too eager to make this point. It was difficult to tell. Drummond was too practiced a politician, and his expression revealed nothing beyond a slight roseate hue from the quantities of wine he had drunk.

"Speaking of matters artistic reminds me to ask you again the name of the artist who painted those sketches of the marbles you showed us," Kedrington said offhandedly, then added with no qualms about doing so, "My wife thinks she would like to commission one or two for our drawing room."

"The boy's name is Dimitri Metaxis," Drummond said, "but I haven't seen him since he delivered the last one."

"Still in town, do you suppose?"

"Very likely. Try some of the cheaper hotels, although I paid him enough to enable him to let private rooms."

Since Sir John seemed to find nothing amiss in these inquiries, Kedrington did not pursue them and thus risk Drummond's suspicion. He took a last lingering sip of his port and decided to save his other questions for another time.

"I think I would like a smoke and a walk to clear all that wine out of my head," he said. "Then I may look in on Brooks's. Do you care to join me, John?"

"Only as far as the smoke," Sir John replied, rising with Kedrington. "I get rude stares at Brooks's."

"I cannot imagine that so ephemeral an insult would have an effect on you."

"It does not, but I only provoke them when I wish to annoy someone, and tonight—thanks to you, dear boy—I am in too mellow a mood to wish to annoy anyone. Even Fenton."

Lord Fenton was a prominent member of White's and a well-known rival of Sir John Drummond, although he sat in the Lords, not the Commons. Kedrington knew the earl only slightly, but was well aware that he considered himself a necessary gadfly, to keep politicians he opposed on the straight and narrow path.

"I expect you could throw him a leveller merely by being civil to him," Kedrington said, as they left the club and strolled off down the street. He offered Drummond one of his Spanish cigarillos, which was accepted, and presently the gentlemen turned on King Street in the direction of St. James's Square, which they circumnavigated slowly while finishing their smokes.

"You should quiz Fenton about the marbles, you know," Drummond said when they were on the point of parting company. "He is firmly in the repatriation camp—the only man in town who still supports Hugh Hammersley's views on returning the so-called bribe paid to Elgin as well as the marbles themselves."

"Hammersley's amendment to the bill of purchase was laughed out of the House."

"No one laughs at Fenton. He is too quick to avenge any perceived slight."

Leaving Kedrington with this thought, Drummond flagged down a hackney coach and departed. The viscount stood on the pavement for a moment longer in a meditative mood, then made up his mind and turned back in the direction they had come. He would look in on Brooks's after all and keep his ears open.

It was with a discouraging sense of having widened the possibilities rather than narrowed them that Kedrington returned home at a late hour. He had consumed no more wine and had consequently had a run of luck at the gaming tables, but his talk with Lord Fenton had been less profitable. Fenton, it turned out, was a fanatic on the subject of the marbles, having once spent six months in Athens as a minor embassy official and now imagining he shared the feelings of the Greeks toward their national treasure. His diatribe on the subject had shed a great deal of heat but little light, and Kedrington had parted from him with the sensation that anyone, even the heavy-handed Fenton, could be behind the mysterious disappearance of two of the sculptures.

On that subject, however, he had heard not a whisper. If anyone had any knowledge of it, he was not a member of Brooks's.

A light tap on his dressing room door as he removed his coat was followed by his wife, in a whisper of silk robes and light perfume. She rose on her toes to kiss him.

"You do smell nastily of smoke," she said, wrinkling her nose. "Have you been drinking as well? What a debaucher you are."

"I have been as sober as a lord."

"You mean, a judge."

"No, I mean the upper classes have been maligned about their drinking habits. The judiciary, on the other hand . . ."

"Do stop talking nonsense. What have you been doing that you could not come home for dinner?"

"I told Trotter not to expect me."

"Which intrigues me all the more. You *planned* to go on a debauche tonight."

Kedrington took off his boots, with his wife's help, and

then reached into his pockets to withdraw a wad of banknotes.

"Here—buy yourself something."

"You've been gaming as well?" Antonia sat down on the edge of his bed to count the money. Kedrington sat down on the other side and pulled her toward him.

"Only in the spirit of inquiry. Besides, I won."

"So I see. You must have been sober."

"The point is, no one else was."

"Is that lesson of the day?"

"Play your cards close to the vest and buy drinks all around. Talk less and listen more. I had dinner with Sir John Drummond, by the way."

"Ah! I knew you suspected him in this affair."

They both knew which affair she referred to and wasted no time in confirming it.

"*You* suspected him. But I cannot say I have ruled him out. He admits quite freely to having employed Dimitri Metaxis, although I believe him when he says he has had no further contact with him. There is also Lord Fenton and his cronies."

"A conspiracy!"

He laughed. "A possibility, although I cannot see Fenton involving himself in anything so sordid. He is a wily fox, despite his bluster."

"Dearest . . ."

"Yes, my life?"

"Who *is* Lord Fenton?"

He told her, briefly, and could almost see the mental note she made to consult his Aunt Julia about it. He hoped she would. Julia welcomed her company, and she loved an intrigue.

"Do you want to know what I did today?"

"Tell me."

She did, and he listened with interest to her observations about Arthur Melville and sat up when she arrived at Dimitri Metaxis.

"Grillon's! Good heavens, I should have thought myself

to make inquiries at all the likely hotels. It even occurred to Sir John before it did to me."

"You cannot be expected to think of everything, dearest. That is why you have me."

"To supply me with ideas? I assure you, my love, I have all sorts of ideas."

"About me?" she asked, snuggling a little closer. He kissed her nose.

"About you," he whispered into her ear. "Would you like to hear some of them?"

"Yes, please."

And so he told her.

Chapter 14

~

Claiming neglect on her husband's part, Lady Kedrington cajoled him into escorting her to the theater the following night to see Edmund Kean in *Macbeth*.

"You need not employ your feminine wiles on me," he told her, "although I am delighted when you do. I am rather fond of the Scottish play, if for no other reason than that it is comparatively short."

"Unless, of course, Mr. Kean repeats his best speeches twice, which Charlotte Overton tells me he occasionally does."

Kedrington promised not to applaud, in order not to encourage London's most celebrated thespian to reiterate himself.

"Was this jaunt Lady Overton's idea, by any chance?"

"Yes, why?"

"I have always suspected her of harboring a secret urge to tread the boards."

"No, how can you think so? She is respectability enshrined."

"Have you never had a secret desire to do something that would outrage your family? Oh, no, I beg your pardon—I forgot that you were fond of splashing about in public fountains and such in your youth."

Antonia rapped her fan on his sleeve. "You promised not to bring that up, and yet you continually do. I should have insisted on having your promise written into the marriage vows. Besides, that was before I met you."

They had descended to the front hall in anticipation of meeting their neighbors, Sir William and Lady Overton, to set out for Drury Lane. Antonia was wearing a new gown with contrasting bodice and skirt, the latter white, with gold spangles around the hem, and the former gold, with a low-cut back, which she turned to display to her husband.

"Very fashionable, I'm sure," he said, contemplating the graceful curve of his wife's spine, "but you will forgive me if I stand behind you—to keep the breeze off, that is."

"I shall carry a shawl," she said saucily, arranging this nearly transparent garment over her shoulders. "Anyway, I want you where I can see you, for you look particularly handsome tonight."

"Thank you, my love," he said, bowing and, Antonia thought, preening a little. Really, he *was* the most hand-some man she knew, even if he looked like a brigand at times and a tulip of the *ton* at others. His black hair and startlingly light eyes always disconcerted one—or at least, Antonia—when one began to take them for granted.

Sir William and his wife were announced just then, and Charlotte was instantly captivated by Antonia's gown and exclaimed delightedly over it. She was some twenty years older than Antonia, but they were friends because Lady Overton had a remarkably youthful outlook on life. She was always interested in the latest mode, even though her own stout figure precluded her wearing anything but the simplest cuts and most conservative colors, and she kept abreast of changing fashions in every other aspect of London life as well. She was a fount of information on any such subject, particularly when it came to the opera and dramatic presentations.

Indeed, when they were seated in their box a short time later, waiting for the play to begin, she confirmed that as a girl, she had indeed longed for a theatrical career.

"Naturally, my mama was horrified and promptly sent me to an extremely reputable academy for young ladies to have proper behavior drilled into me. The head of the school assured Mama that I would learn only the accepted classics in addition to deportment and watercoloring, which would have been discouraging in the extreme."

Antonia agreed, saying she had been fortunate to have an adventurous father and a clever governess.

"Happily," Lady Overton went on, "I had one mistress who slipped me copies of Molière's and Shakespeare's plays, and another who taught me popular tunes on the pianoforte. Poor Mama never found out, but my schoolmates and I had jolly times acting out all the parts and accompanying ourselves with music."

Amused, Antonia said, "You are fortunate, then, that Sir William is not of the same mind as your mama."

"Oh, no, for I should not have married him had that been the case. But he says a season's box at all the theaters is a small price to pay for a happy wife and a comfortable life."

The first act began then, and Antonia saw that Lady Overton's interest was not only in attending the theater but in actually attending to what was happening on stage. During the first interval, indeed, she demonstrated a deep knowledge of the play and an appreciation of Mr. Kean's performance that impressed Antonia. She glanced back at her husband and found him listening with interest as well.

During the second interval, the gentlemen went out to procure refreshments for the ladies, and Lady Overton took up another topic.

"You have not yet been blessed with children, Antonia dear, I know, so I will not bore you with the exploits of my own, but I received a letter from my youngest daughter today, and I am bursting to tell someone that I am shortly to be a grandmother!"

"Why . . . how wonderful for you, Charlotte." Antonia, not expecting this subject to arise, made an effort nonetheless to share her companion's joy. "Is this your first—that is, your other children are not married?"

"Two of them are—I have three, you know—but my oldest boy has been married only a few months, so Anna is the first to be blessed."

She went on in this vein for several minutes, assuming that Antonia knew all about childbirth and raising children, and appeared not to notice that her companion had very little to contribute to the discussion. Antonia found herself listening avidly but at the same time hoping the conversation would not come around to her own expectations.

Unfortunately, Lady Overton had not exhausted her interest in the subject when the curtain went up for the next act, and at the next interval, Antonia quickly asked her husband to take her for a walk around the rotunda.

"Are you feeling unwell, my love?" he asked. "We need not stay for the entire performance if you do not wish to."

"Oh, no, thank you, Duncan. I am perfectly well now. I was only tired of sitting still. I am enjoying the performance," she assured him, although she could not recall a word of the third act.

An acquaintance hailed Kedrington just then, so Antonia made her way to the ladies' retiring room to splash a little cold water on her face, which felt unusually flushed. Fortunately, she encountered a friend there whose own countenance was turning pink, an odd circumstance that piqued Antonia's curiosity sufficiently to enable her to put aside her own distress.

Maria Sefton was rarely discomposed by anyone, however boorish or unpleasant, and indeed, the lady with whom Antonia saw her now would not have struck her as causing any kind of distress in so accomplished a diplomat as Maria Sefton. The other woman was tall and thin, striking rather than beautiful, but Antonia had to admire her regal manner, which doubtless drew both masculine and feminine admiration. She herself had long since given up wishing for more inches and the ability to command respect as well as affection, but she could not help admiring these qualities in other women. And yet, Lady Sefton—Antonia did not think she was mistaken—most definitely disliked the woman.

Curiosity overcame self-consciousness, and as Antonia

accepted the moistened cloth the attendant offered her, she watched the other women out of the corners of her eyes. She examined herself in the glass and rearranged the folds of her gown, scarcely seeing the image that looked back at her as she unashamedly listened to their conversation.

But she could make out no more than a few words, and she was about to leave when Lady Sefton exclaimed, in an artificially high voice, "Oh, there is Lady Kedrington! Do forgive me, Lady Fenton, while I have a few words with her. Perhaps we may meet after the next act . . . ?"

She did not sound as if this prospect pleased, but the other woman agreed, as if nothing would delight her more. She shot a glance at Antonia as she left the withdrawing room, and Antonia was surprised at the cold calculation in her eye, which scarcely matched the honey in her voice.

"*Who*," Antonia said to Lady Sefton when the door had closed behind the other woman, "was *that?*"

Maria sighed. "Lady Fenton. A most disagreeable and trying woman. I wish I could be rude to her, but you may be sure she would spread the tale all over town, *not* to my credit."

Fenton? Antonia frowned. Where had she heard that name recently?

"What did she want?" Antonia asked, inserting her arm companionably into her friend's and strolling back into the foyer of the theater with her.

"She is determined to become a great political hostess, and for some unaccountable reason thinks I can help her. As you know, my dear Antonia, I am not ignorant of politics, but I do not choose my friends on that basis, nor do I organize my own entertainments around that subject. But I think what I particularly dislike about Helen—I beg her pardon, she prefers *Helène* nowadays—is her motives, though I am glad to say they are not entirely clear to me. I should hate to think my mind works the same way."

Antonia smiled at this increasingly peevish diatribe. "No one would ever accuse you, my dear, of being . . . er, having underhand motives."

Lady Sefton sighed. "Well, it is not that precisely. She is nothing if not candid. But I think what I dislike is that all her ambition is for herself—and her husband, presumably—but not to improve the lot of anyone else."

"All ladies should be ambitious for their husbands," said Lord Kedrington, joining them just in time to hear this snippet of conversation. "Would you care for a glass of lemonade, Lady Sefton?"

"My dear Duncan, the very thing," Lady Sefton exclaimed, accepting the cup he held out to her with a grateful sigh. His lordship bowed, murmured, "My pleasure to be of service," and handed the second cup to his wife. He then raised one eyebrow inquiringly at her expression.

"May I ask whose reputation we are cutting to shreds? May anyone join in the game, or is it reserved for ladies?"

Lady Sefton laughed and said she did not dare to think what license to be cutting would produce from Lord Kedrington, but Antonia, who could venture a guess, interrupted to ask if it was not nearly time for the next act.

"Indeed, yes," his lordship said, affecting his tulip of the *ton* manner. "May we escort you back to your box, Lady Sefton?"

"Thank you, Duncan, but I shall find my own way. I do thank you, however—and you, too, Antonia—for the refreshment." She gave Antonia a light hug. "Indeed, I feel quite myself again," she said and left them with a smile.

As they returned to their own box, Antonia gave her husband an abbreviated account of the little incident in the ladies' withdrawing room, and asked what he made of it, but he claimed to have no opinion.

"When you say that, I know you are only working out your opinion in your mind. You will tell me what it is when you come to it, won't you?"

He smiled. "Do I not always tell you what is on my mind?"

"Well, I don't know, do you? If you keep it in your mind, I will never know if you haven't told me."

He smiled and borrowed her opera glasses to survey the boxes opposite them.

"Do you see the Fentons?" Antonia asked.

"Yes. They seem to be with a party of friends, so perhaps you will not be bothered by them again tonight."

"*I* was not bothered, only poor Maria. But I did think it curious that Lady Fenton should have struck up a conversation like that." She frowned and looked thoughtfully into the darkening theater.

He put the glasses down and looked at her. "But something has cut up your peace, my love. What is it?"

She kissed his cheek and answered brightly, "Why, nothing at all. You are imagining it, for how could I not be content here, with my husband to dance attendance on me and two good friends to make a comfortable evening?"

"I am relieved to hear it."

He did not raise the subject again, for which Antonia was grateful, for even she could not put her finger on what was causing her discontent.

Later that night, however, he said, "Have you thought where you would like to go when we leave town next month, my love? If you do not care for Brighton or Worthing, we might go somewhere less crowded—another seaside town, perhaps, or even the West Country."

"That would be nice," Antonia murmured, already half asleep in his arms. He kissed the top of her head.

"Good night, my love. Sleep tight."

He left her then to retire to his own room, but found he could not sleep. He rose and went down to his study, where he lit a candle, trimmed a pen nib, and began making notes on a sheet of paper. It had once been his habit to do this when he was working out a problem, but since his marriage, he had been able to confine this practice to the workings of his country estate. Even that required little enough concentration, and in an odd way, he found that reverting to this practice now, when several genuine difficulties called for resolution, soothed as well as sharpened his mind.

On the first sheet of paper, he wrote:

Marbles.
Persons with access to them.
Persons with the means to remove them.
Persons with a motive to do so.

When, however, he had completed this list, he found that no one name fitted all three categories. He began again from another direction:

Dimitri Metaxis.
Greek patriot organization—leaders?
Arthur Melville.
Sir John Drummond.

He thought for a moment, then added another name:

Lord Fenton.

Chapter 15

~

L ady Kedrington was surprised to find her brother still at the breakfast table when she descended at ten o'clock the next morning en route to an appointment with Cloris Beaumont to look into the Bond Street shops, Antonia not having forgotten her husband's windfall from the gaming tables. She rather fancied a new writing desk for her room and hoped Cloris would not find such a purchase too boring.

"Good morning, slugabed," she said to Carey, posing picturesquely in the doorway, her pert bonnet at a rakish angle and her green spotted muslin walking dress falling elegantly from a rounded neckline. From her shoulders a Norwich shawl hung negligently. "I believe you have not appeared in this plaza for some time, sir."

Carey grinned. "You picked that up from Duncan, didn't you? Did he tell you about the time we watched that bullfight in Zamora right under the nose of the French commandant?"

Antonia shivered. "No, and I do not believe I care to hear it now, however distant the event may be. What are you doing here, Carey?"

She sat down across from him at the table and observed him eating with gusto a large helping of eggs and sausage. She felt slightly queasy just contemplating such a repast. He appeared not to notice and went on eating while he talked.

"What do you mean, what am I doing here? You offered me a room, which I slept in last night, so I assumed the offer was still open."

"Of course it was. I only meant, we have not seen you lately. Where have you been?"

He hesitated, looking as if he had boxed himself into a corner without realizing it.

"You're looking very fetching in that outfit, love," he said, in what his sister recognized as a diversionary tactic. If she did not bring him to heel at once, he would be asking next how she had enjoyed the theater.

"You are not as accomplished a prevaricator as Duncan, nor such a flatterer that I will come all over missish when you tell me how beautiful I am," she told him.

"I meant it!"

She reached out and patted his hand. "Thank you, dear. Now, what have you been up to?"

He broke off a piece of toast, spread creamed eggs on it, and swallowed both before he replied. "Only helping Robin Campbell on guard duty—you know, the marbles."

"Yes, I know. Why does he need more help?"

Carey glared at her. "You *have* been learning from Duncan."

She fluttered her eyelashes at him. "I am only being my usual candid self."

He laughed. "You're incorrigible."

She did not reply to that, knowing in what misdirections it could lead, and finally he could maintain the silence no longer.

"There may perhaps have been another . . . a theft of another . . . some . . . of the marbles."

"*May* have been? Even you could not be so oblivious as to miss *several* large pieces of marble. How many have disappeared since the first one?"

"Well, they aren't precisely missing."

"I know all about that—they have been replaced by replicas. How many is it now?"

"Four in all. But look, Tonia, you won't tell Duncan I told you, will you?"

"What? Oh . . . no, not if you don't wish me to."

"That's a relief."

"Unless he asks me directly, of course. I never lie to him."

"Tonia!"

She added ruefully, "I'd never get away with it." Seeing Carey's stricken expression, however, she soothed him with, "I'm sure he'd never think to ask me, love. Why should he? Anyway, you're going to tell him, aren't you? Or are you leaving it to poor Mr. Campbell to break the news?"

Carey squirmed a bit in his chair and conceded that he would have to tell Kedrington.

"He hasn't gone out already, has he?" he asked, half hoping she would say he had gone to Burlington House and Carey had just missed him.

"I believe he's still in the stables. One of the horses we took last night has gone lame, and he wanted to consult the groom about it. You'd best look for him there."

He sighed and rose to do so, but Antonia took his sleeve for a moment. "Carey, you will be careful, won't you? And look out for Duncan too? We don't know how desperate the people behind this scheme may be."

This succeeded in putting him in a position to reassure her, which improved his spirits markedly. He was at heart a chivalrous man, Antonia reflected with a smile.

"Don't worry, Tonia," he said, patting her hand avuncularly. "Even if there's trouble lurking, we can take care of ourselves."

This did not reassure her as he might have hoped, but she smiled gratefully nonetheless and promised herself not to give in to her apprehensions.

"I shall be off then. Will you be home for dinner by any chance?"

"'Fraid not, love. Duty calls and all."

"Of course. And the company at Boodle's is much more agreeable, I have no doubt."

She left him protesting that it was no such thing, but she was glad that he had not once mentioned Elena, or apparently even thought of her, for his melancholy of the last fortnight had left him. She hoped this was a good thing. She hoped it did not indicate that he no longer thought of Elena and that she was therefore wrong in working toward a reconciliation.

Antonia left the house in renewed contemplation.

A few hours in the company of Cloris Beaumont, however, was more than enough to make Antonia merry again. After making several extravagant purchases each, the ladies repaired for a refreshing stroll through the Green Park, followed at a discreet distance by one of the Kedringtons' footmen.

"Does he go everywhere you do?" Cloris asked, smiling coyly and giving a little wave at the young man, who remained straight-faced. "He's rather sweet."

Antonia laughed. "William would blush to the roots of his hair to hear you say so. And no, he does not follow me everywhere, but he is under orders from Duncan to protect me, so I do allow him to carry out his duty in public places. Were I to trip and break some joint, for example, he would come in handy for carrying me back to the carriage."

Cloris imagined the possibilities. "I wonder what the Beau would think to see me carried back to Cavendish Square in the arms of a handsome young man."

"Baggage! Why do you tease him so?"

"Because I can—without fearing that he will tear his hair out in despair or fall into a jealous rage."

"I expect you had quite enough of that sort of behavior from your swains before you were married."

"Yes, it became tiresome rather quickly. The good thing about the Beau—one of many, I hasten to say—is that his feathers are never ruffled by trivialities. He reserves his feelings for more important matters."

Antonia wondered what matters might be important enough to disturb Edmund Beaumont's seemingly imperturbable calm. She supposed he must have displayed warm feelings when he was courting Cloris—and afterward too, of course, for Cloris did not appear unhappy in her marriage. Indeed, she had benefited from the union in subtle ways which she might not recognize herself. She no longer spoke in breathless italics designed to draw attention to herself, her taste in clothes had softened, and she no longer cared to be called Clory, her universal nickname since her schooldays.

"Have you received a letter from Isabel this week?" Antonia asked, following this line of thought.

"Only yesterday," Cloris told her. "I must say, I am glad she has not let our friendship fade, as it did after we left school and before we met again during our season. I am not nearly so prolific a letter writer as she is, but happily she does not expect an answer to every letter."

"She cannot be so active as she was, given her delicate condition. I daresay she enjoys being able to sit at home and read and write letters." Antonia smiled at the mental picture she conjured up of her niece ensconced in the library window at Wyckham, where she herself once dreamily contemplated the gentle Leicestershire hills.

"She always was bookish," Cloris observed, putting up her parasol as they passed from under the trees into the sunlit walkway. "It is as well that the Beau is not so. He plays chess with his cronies, however, which is almost as bad, for I am not allowed to disturb him during a match. Still—our occupations do not conflict, for when he is thus engaged, I may go out and buy fripperies!"

Antonia only half listened to this speech, her mind being still on her niece and her coming confinement. Would it be a boy or a girl? Antonia rather hoped for a girl, but Isabel had never expressed a preference.

They passed a bench occupied by two nannies who gossiped while their charges played together on the grass. A boy and a girl. Which would Duncan prefer? One of each would be best, of course, and she supposed there must be an heir before she could indulge in a little girl. But what if there could be only one . . . ? Or even . . .

"Let us go back, shall we?" she said abruptly. "I find I am more tired than I thought."

"Of course," Cloris agreed readily. If she sensed her companion's change of mood, she did not reveal it. She did, however, continue talking until they reached the gate, in such a way that Antonia was not obliged to say more than yes or no.

It was just as they passed through the gate that Antonia saw someone in the distance who succeeded in turning her mind in another direction.

"Elena!"

"Where?" Cloris said. "Do you mean Carey's Elena? Do introduce me. I have not met her, you know, since she did not appear at your dinner party."

Antonia took William aside to instruct him to detain Miss Melville. He crossed the street and, stepping in front of Elena, said something that made her stop and turn to look in the direction he indicated. Antonia thought she saw a fleeting look of panic cross Elena's face, but the clever footman had positioned himself in such a way that she could not flee without knocking him down and causing a scene. She apparently realized this, and finally smiled and waved in Antonia's direction. William then escorted her across the street, and by the time she reached Antonia and Cloris, she seemed to have let down her guard.

"Elena, dear, what a happy accident!" Antonia said quickly, but in the normal cordial tones of ladies well acquainted with one another. "I should like to introduce you to another friend, Mrs. Beaumont. She was at school with my niece, as I may not have mentioned to you."

"How do you do?" Elena said, holding out her hand. Cloris, accustomed to embracing other ladies, even those she did not know intimately, hesitated for a moment, and then took Elena's hand, smiling warmly.

"I'm pleased to meet you," Cloris said primly, and Antonia let out her breath. She was not going to mention Carey's name, bless her. Cloris did say, inevitably, "Antonia has told me *so* much about you."

Elena blushed slightly and murmured something about Lady Kedrington's extreme kindness.

"We were just going to Gunter's for ices," Antonia announced, raising Cloris's brows inquiringly, as nothing had been said about the matter before this moment. "Won't you join us? I find the air is warmer today than I had anticipated, despite the breeze, and walking has quite sapped my strength. I should like something cool."

Elena hesitated, but Cloris leapt in to add her urgings, and before Miss Melville was aware of it, she had been helped up into Lady Kedrington's carriage, which had magically appeared in the street, and was soon seeing Piccadilly from a different vantage point.

"I suppose we will think about removing to the country soon," Antonia said, for the sake of saying something, as they made their way through the traffic. "Summer will soon be on us, and as uncaring as we are for convention, there *is* good reason for not remaining in town during the hottest part of the year."

"I rather enjoy the heat," Elena said. "But perhaps I am constitutionally more adapted to it."

"You were born in Greece, were you not?" Cloris inquired. "I expect it is very hot there in the summer."

The conversation continued along these insipid lines up Berkeley Street to the square, and while Antonia—and certainly Cloris—would have screamed in frustration at it in the normal way, it did serve to put Elena more at ease, so that when their carriage stopped in front of the confectioner's shop, she was almost animated.

Even the appearance just then of Hester Coverley did not seem to dismay her. Indeed, Elena smiled—more at Hester's feathered bonnet than delight at seeing her, no doubt—when Hester said how glad she was that she happened to be on her way home just at that moment, and was Antonia coming to call.

That made Antonia glance toward the other side of the square, wondering if Julia could see them. Hester interpreted her look, saying, "If you were not coming to visit, Antonia dear, do not be concerned. Julia cannot see across the square from her window in summer—although I vow she would cut down the trees in order to do so if she were allowed, but even Julia could not gain permission for that!"

Antonia laughed and, disclaiming any reason to hide from Julia Wilmot, invited Hester to join them in the carriage, which Hester did, plumping herself down beside Elena and continuing the steam of gossip and small talk in which she customarily indulged when not restrained by Julia Wilmot's dampening presence.

It was the custom for ladies to remain in their carriages under the leafy shade of Berkeley Square while Gunter's waiters came out to them to take their orders. Their party, however, was honored by the proprietor himself, who recognized an aristocratic patroness when he saw one and hurried eagerly to do her bidding. Cloris and Antonia had fruit ices, and Hester a lemonade, but Elena selected only a single apricot tart from a tray presented to her.

"You are fortunate, my lady," their host said, addressing Antonia, "that we have only yesterday received a cargo of ice from the Greenland seas and are able to offer you the best summer fruit made into delectable cooling delicacies. You will find your raspberry and pineapple ices particularly delectable—an excellent choice indeed."

He hovered, extolling his wares, for just a shade under the time when he might have become a nuisance, and then left the ladies to their treats. When he had disappeared inside his shop again, Elena whispered, "Where do they keep the ice so it does not melt?"

"In the cellars," Hester told her. "I was once given a tour of the premises, and I can tell you it is very cold in that cellar—like winter in July."

"You really should have had a sorbet, Elena," Antonia said. "Mr. Gunther takes pride in his recipe, which is as much a secret as any state document."

"Another time, perhaps," she said, which pleased Antonia, who interpreted this as a promise that Elena would not disdain her friendship after all, despite the present delicate situation between them. She decided that she could wait to question Elena on sensitive subjects, despite her strong inclination to do so while she had the bird in hand; if she fled to the bush, the opportunity might be lost.

She was rewarded for her patience later when, after bidding farewell to Hester and dropping Cloris at Cavendish Square, the carriage proceeded to Marylebone to convey Elena to her home.

Antonia did not descend from the carriage, as Elena had not invited her inside. As they said their farewells on the pavement, Elena suddenly clutched Antonia's hand and said, "Do you forgive me, then, dear Lady Kedrington?"

"Of course," Antonia began, flustered. "That is, there is nothing to forgive!"

"There is," Elena said. "There are reasons . . ."

She looked up at the house as if fearful of being spied upon, and Antonia almost lost her patience with all these hints and intimations and demanded to know what those reasons were that made them so important that her brother's heart might be broken because of them.

But then Elena said, "May I call on you?"

Antonia breathed a quick sigh of relief, smiled, and kissed her on the cheek. "Whenever you wish, Elena, dear."

"Thank you," Elena whispered, then turned to hurry up the steps to her door. She reached it as it was being opened to her, and did not look back.

It was only when Elena had disappeared inside the house that Antonia remembered that she had entirely forgotten to ask about the subject she had been burning with curiosity about—the mysterious Dimitri.

She leaned out the window and called up, "Albemarle Street, please."

She would surprise her quarry in his own lair.

Chapter 16

Robin Campbell sat in the sturdiest of the two chairs in his office with his bad leg up on the table that served him as a desk. Lord Kedrington had abandoned the chair when his friend entered, his limp markedly more pronounced, and had insisted that he rest the leg by making it do no more work.

"I can give it a rub, if you like," Kedrington said, sitting on the edge of the desk and laying his hand experimentally on Robin's knee. "I'm quite accomplished at getting the kinks out of sore limbs, having suffered milder forms of your complaint myself. Did I tell you I got a knife in the thigh once?"

"Carey told me that one," Robin said, making no protest at Kedrington's ministrations, which the viscount interpreted as a sure sign that Robin was in severe pain.

"And what have you been doing to aggravate your injury?" Kedrington asked, feeling gently above Robin's boot. Robin finally opened his mouth to protest, but Kedrington gave him a look that stayed the words in his throat. He then proceeded to pull off the boot and began gently massaging the tight muscles in calf and knee until Robin visibly relaxed.

"Well?"

"Chasing villains."

Kedrington raised his brows. "How intrepid of you! Which villains?"

Robin smiled. "Actually, only one. And we cannot be certain as yet that he is a villain—Dimitri Metaxis."

"Tell me."

"I was assigned to place an order with a certain packing firm in Long Acre for the manufacture of the special cases that the marbles will eventually be moved in. Incidentally, I tried to give the business to Hollister, but it was not my decision to make. Anyway, it occurred to me after I had left the place that I should have asked if anyone had brought in a similar order recently—to establish how the fakes were put in place—and just before I reached the shop for the second time, I saw Metaxis come out of it. As you may imagine, I was surprised to see him."

Kedrington smiled at the understatement. "Did he see you?"

"Unfortunately, yes. I came to a dead halt in the middle of the street, where there was no place to hide. He ran off, and I tried to follow him, but he easily outdistanced me."

"He recognized you, then?"

"I can't be sure of that. But it must have been obvious that I recognized *him*. I don't suppose he was eager to be properly introduced."

"Did you find out what he wanted in the shop?"

"That was my next move, having failed to intercept Metaxis to question him directly. I went back to the shop, and the proprietor told me that a gentleman had just been in to inquire about the same cases I had just ordered—or not precisely. The proprietor checked the records again, and it transpired that his clerk had taken a similar order just that morning. It was that order which Metaxis had inquired about."

Kedrington frowned. "So Dimitri did not *place* the order?"

"Apparently not. But there was no name or address on the order form, only a signature that was merely a scrawl—impossible to read."

"Deliberately so, I imagine."

"So I supposed. The clerk had been sent on an errand, so

I could not question him directly as to what the person who placed the order looked like. He paid ahead, in gold, so the clerk apparently did not ask any pertinent questions. The goods were to be picked up when they were ready."

"It appears we shall have to put a watch on the shop as well, although I dislike spreading the men so thinly."

"I doubt it will yield any information. Metaxis knows he has been spotted there."

"True, but if he did not place the order, the person who did would come back to collect the goods. I believe we can . . . er, persuade the proprietor to keep an eye out for us. Further, if what I am beginning to suspect is true, and Dimitri is not in league with the thieves—at least not directly—then he would not tell them he had been spotted. They may come back unsuspecting."

He leaned back against the wall opposite the table and rubbed his chin thoughtfully. Robin looked perplexed.

"I'm not sure I follow that."

Kedrington straightened and reached for his hat. "Never mind. I think I shall pay a call at the shop myself. Perhaps I can save ourselves the drudgery of watching the shop, as well as Grillon's, by greasing a few palms."

"Who's watching Grillon's now?"

"Lieutenant Fairfax. I thought it was safe to put him on during the day. I suspect that Metaxis works by night and more than likely sleeps the day through."

"Will you be back here tonight?"

"Sooner than that, I hope. We need to gather the other men to put our plan in motion to catch the thieves before yet another piece disappears. But first, there is something I need to look into."

"What?"

"If I tell you, you'll do it for me."

"Of course, if I can."

"You can't, so don't ask. Rest for now."

Duncan left the room, closing the door behind him to cut off any protest Robin might make. He did not intend to put any of his friends in danger or even discomfort if he could help it, so the less Robin knew ahead of time, the better.

What he had found to explore was a passageway into the bowels of the building—or to be precise, he imagined, into the underground area originally excavated for some other building, whose construction had been halted while the marbles remained in their temporary structure above them. The likelihood was that "temporary" would last no more than another month or six weeks, but that was more than enough time to remove all the original marbles, if that was what the plotters intended, and if they were not apprehended before they could carry their plans any further.

The viscount returned to Burlington House two hours later, having frustrated himself in one quest but made better progress with another. He had first gone to several locations in the more fashionable parts of London with the intent to try the mysterious key he had taken from the dead man in the less fashionable East End—and had ended cursing his own impulse to take it.

He had been somewhat more successful in impressing the foreman of the men who loaded packing goods for shipment from the warehouse in back of the Long Acre shop with his rank and ready money into revealing the names of certain of the shop's clients. He was not entirely certain that the man believed the tale he had spun about urgent government business requiring the utmost discretion, but the blunt he was prepared to part with was enough to tighten the lip of even the most suspicious foreman.

He decided against announcing his return to Burlington House, however, until after he had a chance to make his explorations of the underground area of the building. Thus, he slipped into the rear entrance, using his copy of the key Robin had given him, and from there stole around the back of the display area to a door half hidden behind the largest friezes.

It was not, he noted, a large enough opening to bring even the relatively small horses' heads from the corners of the east pediment through, so there must be other doors invisible from the outside. He would need to find those.

He closed the door softly behind him, but remained in the dark for only a moment. Finding his way by touch, he located the lantern he had earlier hung on the wall inside and lighted it.

He was inside a passage that seemed to run the length of the building above in approximately a northerly direction. He continued with silent steps along the passage, running his hand along the outer wall. Presently, he came to a set of shelves built into the wall and containing only some broken pieces of plaster, apparently the remains of the decorations of some other house, or perhaps an earlier version of Burlington House itself.

Kedrington ran his hand along the shelves and around the sides until he came to a hole concealed behind a packing case, which he was easily able to shift. He put his hand into the hole and felt, with satisfaction, a latch on the other side. He pushed it up, and the whole wall of shelving opened slightly inward.

A glance at the outline of this new door told him that when fully opened into the area behind, it was more than large enough to accommodate the first frieze that had gone missing, but he did not open it fully. Instead, he opened it only wide enough to slip through, then closed the door behind him.

He was now in what looked like the yard of a posting inn, except that it was entirely enclosed by what must appear from the outside like the side of a warehouse. Before him, the ground sloped downward slightly, and what would have been the carriage entrance to the inn disappeared under the floor of the structures above, some two hundred yards ahead of him.

He walked down the road, noting footprints and wheel tracks in the dust beneath his feet. He wondered what had been in this part of London centuries ago—an inn? a house in medieval times? The question interested him, but he dismissed it from his mind for later academic study. Now he must concentrate on where he was going.

Under where the adjacent building met the one he had entered from, the ceiling was lower, but the road wider, lined on top by supporting beams and on either side by wooden pillars. Behind those, a narrow foot passage paralleled the roadway.

He stopped to examine the supports, wondering idly what was above them. He pulled out a compass to orient himself; he would have to explore the street next, to see what buildings adjoined that which held the marbles.

He heard a noise just then and went still. He listened for a moment, but heard nothing more. Nonetheless, he blew out the lantern and went still again, listening.

Then he heard them, barely audible on the soft earth.

Footsteps.

Chapter 17

❧

L
ady Kedrington descended from her carriage in front
of Grillon's Hotel, uncertain what to do next.

"You may go," she said to the coachman, who
looked as if he would refuse to leave her there alone, so she
added, "Return for me in twenty minutes."

Still looking doubtful, the coachman nonetheless did as
he was bade and drove off. The concierge, recognizing
quality even when it did not arrive in a crested conveyance,
bowed and inquired how he might help her.

Antonia smiled sweetly through the veil she had artfully
fashioned on the way to the hotel from the swath of muslin
that had decorated her hat.

"I am to meet my cousin here," she whispered in a
breathless tone, which she hoped would both disguise her
voice and give the doorman the impression that she had an
assignation about which she wished him to remain discreet. She pressed a coin into his hand to emphasize this
point.

"Certainly, my lady," said the doorman, bowing. "Please
go in and inquire at the desk."

She entered by the door he held open to her, and it was
only when she was standing inside the hotel that Antonia
noticed her footman a discreet distance behind her, having
apparently followed her in without her knowledge.

"William!" she whispered.

"My lady?"

"Kindly wait over there." She motioned toward a corner of the lobby half hidden in the shadows.

"May I not make your inquiries for you?" William asked, as reluctant as the coachman to let her out of his sight. Antonia reflected ruefully that she had forgotten how surrounded she was by persons determined to cosset her. That, it seemed, was why Duncan could succeed at his spying, while she could not even make the smallest attempt at it without revealing herself.

"No," she said baldly. "Go away."

Torn between duty and disobedience, William complied, but only so far as the pillar beside the staircase, from where he could still see his mistress, even if she suddenly bolted for the stairs. Antonia approached the desk.

"I am to meet my cousin here," she said to the clerk, repeating her story for lack of a more original one. "His name is Mr. Metaxis."

The clerk eyed her balefully, but appeared to accept that a very fair, obviously English, beauty should be related in any way to a very dark, foreign personage of hitherto solitary habits.

"That gentleman has not yet come down," the clerk told her.

"Oh, then he is in the hotel?"

"Yes, madam. Shall I send a message to his room?"

"Oh, no . . . that is, he knows I will be here. I will wait."

"There is a ladies' parlor through that door, madam."

Antonia glanced in the direction he indicated. "Oh . . . ah, thank you, no. I have my servant with me. I shall wait in that chair over there."

She smiled again and went away quickly when another patron demanded the clerk's attention. She sat down in a large chair, prepared to wait. William moved closer to her, but when she glared at him, he said nothing and moved to stand behind her, where she could not see him. Antonia accepted his presence in a spirit of resignation. And, she was forced to admit to herself, she did feel safer with a familiar guardian.

She soon almost forgot William and was taking a lively interest in the persons who paraded before her field of vision. Grillon's was known as the military man's hotel, but very few of its patrons were actually in uniform. She supposed it had been a different case when they were still at war, but since Waterloo, most of the army had been demobilized, and those who had homes to go to doubtless did.

A woman of middle age but youthful figure, gowned in a striking, if slightly vulgar, emerald green creation, stood speaking with three gentlemen at once. Antonia wondered if she could be what was referred to as an "abbess"—a woman who ran a house of ill repute. She could not be entirely unrespectable, or doubtless she would not have been let into the hotel, which, while not patronized by the *ton*, was not disdained by decent, even distinguished, travelers and diners.

Absorbed in these musings, she was startled when a voice said suddenly, "Tonia! Good God, what are you doing here?"

She looked up to see her brother staring at her.

"Shh! Do sit down, Carey, and stop that racket."

He did so in another large chair that he pulled closer to hers, but went on, "What's that thing you've got over your face? I should not have recognized you."

"That is precisely the object, you widgeon. How *did* you recognize me?"

Carey glanced up at William, but when Antonia turned her head to the footman, he had resumed his bland expression and disinterested manner.

"Traitor!" she muttered.

"Never mind that," Carey said. "Answer my question."

"What question?"

"*Tonia . . . !*"

"Shh! I am looking for Dimitri Metaxis, of course. Isn't that what you are doing here as well?"

"Yes, it is," he said, seizing the point. "Which is why there is no need for you to be sitting about in a public place like a common—"

"Don't even say it. I am no such thing. Besides, however much I discourage him, I do have William."

"Nonetheless—"

"Carey, wait!" she interrupted urgently. "I think I see him! Look over there!"

Carey displayed more subtlety than his sister would have credited him with by looking instead into a long mirror on the wall above their heads. Only when he had confirmed what he saw did he lean toward her and whisper, "Stay where you are until I am out of sight. Then go home."

She opened her mouth to protest, but he added, "Or I'll tell Duncan."

"Oh, very well!" she promised unwillingly.

He rose then, slowly, so as not to draw attention to himself, and turned to face the desk. Unfortunately, just at that moment, the clerk pointed in Antonia's direction, and Metaxis turned and saw them. Antonia looked back at a masculine version of Elena Melville—taller, handsome, his black hair curlier than hers. He glanced from her to Carey, who was standing very still in an effort to blend into the wainscoting, and then abruptly turned and made for a door behind the desk.

"Blast!" said Carey and followed.

Antonia rose, but there was no point in following the two men. There was, for that matter, no longer any point to remaining inside the hotel.

"Come along, William."

She was astonished to discover, upon emerging from the hotel, that less than half an hour must have passed, for her carriage was waiting on the pavement in front of her.

William opened the door for her, but before she stepped up, she said to him, "You may now make yourself truly useful, William, by climbing up on the box and instructing Denby to look for Carey and Mr. Metaxis—that gentleman we saw in the hotel. They cannot have gone far yet."

William, apparently getting into the spirit of the thing at last, did as he was told with alacrity, and shortly they were under way. Antonia raised her veil and looked out the window to discover that they had turned down a narrow alley. She could see nothing ahead of her and only the brick walls of buildings to the sides, so, frustrated, she pulled her head back in again.

At the end of the alley, they paused, then crossed a broader thoroughfare which, Antonia was startled to realize when she glanced out, was Bond Street. Traffic, both vehicular and pedestrian, was much heavier here, and Antonia could distinguish no particular person in the throng. She drew farther back into the carriage to avoid being seen and hoped that William had a better vantage point on the perch.

When the carriage came to a halt a few moments later, however, that hope vanished. William climbed down and came to her window to say that he had seen neither Carey nor "the foreign gentleman" again.

"Where would you be wishful to go now, my lady?"

"Where are we, William?"

"Cork Street, my lady. I saw Mr. Fairfax come this way, but when we turned up the street, he was no longer in sight."

Antonia pondered this a moment, glanced back the way they had come, and said, "I wish to get out."

William obligingly helped her down, then followed as she proceeded up the street, glancing into every doorway and mews she passed. There were houses on only the west side of the street, the east side being occupied by gardens, which effectively limited her search.

Nonetheless, she had found nothing unusual by the time she reached the end of the street. She turned and walked back, looking up this time instead of at doors and alleys at eye level. It was thus that she noticed that one of the last buildings at the south end of the street was unoccupied. There was no knocker on the door, and shades rather than curtains covered all the windows. She looked at this house more carefully, up and down, until she saw something in the dust of the carriage drive. Footprints.

She leaned over slightly and examined them. They seemed to be fresh, as the drive was very dusty and the marks would have blown away had they not been made recently. What was more, the indentations in the dirt were very smooth, indicating leather soles and a fine new pair of boots.

Carey had come this way.

She started forward, but William caught up with her and asked, "Shall I go first, my lady?"

She was about to dismiss him again, but then had another thought. "Thank you, William. I believe Mr. Fairfax came this way. Perhaps you would walk around to the back of this house and see if he is still there."

"Certainly, my lady," William responded, apparently forgetting that he would of necessity leave his mistress standing in the road by herself if he carried out this request, but as Antonia had hoped, that was precisely what he did.

As soon as he had gone, Antonia darted into the shadow of a doorway she had seen at the side of the house. There was no lock on the old wooden double door—she supposed it had once led to stables or some kind of pantry—but when she tried the latch, the door opened. She went in.

She descended two stone steps and found herself in a dark, dirt-floored room, which was apparently empty. There were only two small windows at street level to admit light. She waited for a moment until her eyes grew accustomed to the dark, then explored the perimeter of the wall.

A sound startled her, and she looked up apprehensively at the window, but then realized that it was only William returning from his errand. She supposed she ought to go out before he found her gone and began a search. Reluctantly, she turned toward the door—and stumbled over something on the floor.

She looked down and saw that it was an iron ring, attached to some sort of door. A trapdoor! Dared she open it? Could she? She considered her new gloves for a moment, then took them off, stuffed them into the pocket in her petticoat, and took hold of the ring with both hands.

She had thought the hinges might be rusted shut, but to her surprise, the trapdoor opened readily, as if it had been frequently, and recently, used. This gave her pause again. She looked down into the hole she had revealed and saw the outline of a ladder.

She was mulling over what she would do next when she heard William run past again. Quickly, she pulled up her skirts and scrambled down the ladder, hoping there were not too many cobwebs attached to it.

The last rung of the ladder was farther from the ground than she would have guessed, and she nearly fell, clutching the ladder to prevent herself from doing so. She straightened up and saw that she was now inside some kind of cellar, even darker than the room above, with only the faint light coming through the trapdoor to see by. She listened for a moment, hoping there were no rats here, but the cellar was as clean as such places could be, and apparently empty. She peered into the darkness.

Some distance away, she thought she saw a wooden wall. She ventured closer and touched it. It was not a wall, after all, but some very large packing cases. Something was being stored down here. She felt her way along the wooden sides of the cases until she came to an end. There she felt a slight movement of air and a change in the temperature; the air was cooler here. Slowly, for she could scarcely see at all, she moved forward into what seemed to be some kind of passage.

Then she saw a light ahead of her. A lantern! She began to move toward it, then stopped abruptly. If there was a lantern, there might be someone down here. She moved close to the wall of the passage, out of the direct light.

A voice from out of the dark said in exasperated tones, "I don't believe this."

Startled, Antonia screamed, and a hand clasped itself over her mouth.

"Shh! Antonia, it is I."

She grasped the hand and pulled it away from her face, then inhaled a deep breath. "Duncan!"

He turned her around. "Are you mad? I might have shot you! What in God's name are you doing here?"

It was only then that she saw the pistol in his other hand. Her knees went weak, and she almost fell, but he held her upright.

"How did you know it was me?"

"Your perfume."

"Oh."

"Antonia, what are you doing here? How did you get in?"

She waved vaguely back in the direction she had come. "There was a trapdoor . . . I saw Carey's footprints . . . and what are *you* doing here, Duncan? I thought you were going to see Robin."

"I did. We are under Burlington House—or at least I was when I set out on this little excursion. I'm not certain where I've finished up."

Antonia looked back the way she had come, even though she could see only a few feet back into the passage, and said, "Oh, yes, of course. I was north of . . . oh, dear."

She looked up to find him patiently waiting, his brief burst of anger forgotten, for further explanation. "Dearest, do you think we could go out?" she said. "I expect William is beside himself with worry by now, poor dear."

He sighed and put his pistol back into his coat. "I won't even begin to try to understand that. You can explain it all at home—and then I'll decide whether I must lock you in your room. Of all the foolish, reckless . . ."

He continued to mutter under his breath in this fashion until they reached the room with the ladder. There he stopped abruptly, raised his lantern, and exclaimed, "Good God!"

"Now what?" Antonia said. "Oh, those cases—I could not be sure earlier that was what they were, since I had no light. Do you know what is in them?"

He grinned, then wrapped his free arm around her and kissed her soundly. "Antonia, you are amazing!"

Disentangling herself, she said, "I don't know why people always say that we ladies are flighty and change our minds constantly. If anyone saw you now—"

"Let us hope no one does," Kedrington said, sobering suddenly, "and let us get out of this place before William raises a hue and cry and someone *does* see us. I'll explain when we get home."

"Does that mean you will not lock me in my room?" she said as he helped her up the ladder.

"That still remains to be seen."

Chapter 18

❦

"**I**s it not possible that the marbles were stolen for the sole purpose of returning them to Greece?" Lady Kedrington asked her husband. "I must say, Duncan, your devious mind is capable of imagining a staggering number of the most complicated reasons for the theft, but might it not come down to the simplest of them in the end?"

They were seated in Lord Kedrington's study the day after their adventure in the underground passage, in furtherance of his promise to keep her informed of the progress of what she was pleased to call "our investigation." They had spent the previous night explaining to each other the peculiar circumstances that had brought each of them into the underground passage at the same time—although from opposite ends—but they had fallen asleep before they were able to consider the consequences of what they had found and what action ought to be taken—and by whom.

"It may very well come down to the most obvious answer," he said in defense of his mental habits. "But I like to consider all the possibilities. It is better to start with as many as one can imagine and eliminate them one by one than to be surprised by an unthought-of contingency just when one has become enamored of some other scheme."

"That sounds very profound."

"Only logical. I like to keep an open mind."

"Very well, then," Antonia said, "explain what a political motive might be."

She was comfortably ensconced on a sofa, with her legs curled up beneath the blue satin-striped skirts of her favorite day dress, which was no longer fresh enough to be worn in company, and a cup of chocolate in her hand. She drained the contents and put the cup on the small table beside the sofa, then looked to him for an answer.

"To embarrass the government," he said.

"So it must be someone in the opposition."

"Never say *must* about politicians," Kedrington advised. "It could very well be a member of the prime minister's own party, out to discredit him or some other faction."

"In other words, Sir John Drummond and Lord Fenton are equally likely candidates?"

"Someone *such as* Drummond or Fenton, yes. Outspoken advocates of any position are unlikely to resort to illegal acts to get their way, however, since they would be the first to be suspected."

"But for that reason, they might believe themselves beyond suspicion."

He smiled. "Now you are thinking like a politician."

"Oh, dear, did I really say that? It is all your fault for putting ideas into my head."

"I do enjoy doing so, you know. I can be sure they will not simply rattle around in there with nothing to feed on. Although I insist that you not put your precious person in peril again, you do have a nimble mind, my love, and should use it more."

She leaned over to kiss him. "You say the nicest things."

What he might have said, or done, in reply was cut off by the abrupt entrance into the room, unannounced, of Lady Kedrington's brother.

"See here, Duncan," Carey burst out. "Something's happened that—oh, hullo, Tonia. Didn't know you were in here."

"Could you not have inquired of Trotter if we were receiving visitors?" the viscount asked in aggrieved tones.

"But you don't understand—Elena's disappeared!"

"What?" This caught Antonia's interest at once. "What do you mean, disappeared?"

"Dimitri, too, although the two were not together as far as I can tell. He's left Grillon's at any rate. Paid his shot and departed early this morning."

"How do you *know* Elena is missing?" Antonia asked, having had two seconds to put her nimble mind to work. Her husband smiled encouragingly.

"I told you so," he said, sotto voce.

Carey paid no attention to this exchange, having some difficulty in formulating his reply.

"I met this girl, Mary—"

"Carey!" his sister exclaimed. "Never tell me you have been unfaithful to Elena already!"

"No such thing!" he protested. "I'd never—but that's beside the point."

"What *is* the point?" Kedrington inquired.

"Well, Mary— Her dad owns a flower barrow that he keeps on Gloucester Place and Mary and I got to talking one day, that's all. Anyway, today she told me that Elena got into a carriage yesterday morning and drove away and hasn't come back."

"How does *she* know? I don't suppose she watched the house day and night."

"No, but she went up to the door the next morning and asked for the mistress of the house. The butler told her that everyone was away, the master and his ward both."

"Together?"

"No. Mary asked. And she said it wasn't Melville's carriage Elena got into. She didn't recognize it or see who else was in it. Besides, she'd seen Melville drive off the day before and knew he hadn't come back."

"Observant girl."

"Er, well . . . I asked her to keep a lookout for me. Can't be in six places at once, can I?"

Antonia put her arm around her brother's waist. "Of course you can't, love, and I know you were worried about Elena."

Kedrington gave her a sharp look. "Why should he be?"

"Never mind, dearest. I'll explain it all to you later."

He raised his eyes heavenward in exasperation. "Do you mean we are not finished with explanations yet?"

Antonia disregarded this peevishness and said, "Now I think I must call on Arthur Melville—if he has returned—at once. Carey, will you ask someone to bring the carriage around front? I shan't be more than twenty minutes."

"I'll come, too," Carey said.

"No, you won't," Kedrington returned. "You'll only set up Melville's back if he's there, and if he's not, I think I can get more out of the servants than you could."

Carey surprised them both by agreeing with this and—as a reward, Antonia suspected—Kedrington suggested that he go to the City and inquire at the Swan whether Miss Melville had purchased a ticket for the Mail. If not, he could then attempt to learn what sort of carriage she had left in and try to pick up its trail.

To Antonia, such a search seemed a hopelessly lengthy prospect, but Carey made no demur and, eager to make himself useful, he departed as abruptly as he had arrived.

"That should exhaust him sufficiently," his lordship remarked.

An hour later, the Kedringtons raised the knocker on Arthur Melville's door. It was a moment before it was opened to them by a harried-looking butler. Antonia guessed that his employer had recently returned home and found the household being run not at all to his liking.

This proved to be the case when they were shown into a drawing room, and an equally harried Arthur Melville hurried in to greet them.

"My dear Lady Kedrington, Lord Kedrington, how good of you to call." He shook both their hands and invited them to be seated.

"I imagine you have come to call on Elena, but I regret to inform you that she is not at home. In fact . . . oh, dear, I do not know how to say this . . . I am not precisely sure where she is, as she apparently slipped out without being observed. I don't suppose she has communicated with . . . ?"

"She did not leave any message for you?" Kedrington asked, not answering Melville's question.

Something in his tone alerted Melville. "You knew, then? That she had gone? How, may I ask?"

"My brother was concerned about her, and called earlier," Antonia said soothingly. "You had not yet returned then, so he came to us."

"I see. I was out of town—on business, you understand—until only a short time ago. None of the servants has been able to supply any hint of where she has gone, for she said nothing to any of them about leaving. I was on the point of calling in the Bow Street Runners."

"You should have called on us," Antonia chided him, still in the soothing voice designed to lull him into confiding in her. "We are naturally eager to help."

"Thank you. I would have done so, certainly, but I did not wish to worry you any sooner than necessary. There may be some perfectly simple explanation . . . although I confess I cannot think of one."

Kedrington had been observing his host closely during this exchange and now said, "Would you object to showing us Miss Melville's room? Perhaps we may notice some clue the servants have missed."

Melville hesitated for a moment, then seemed to resign himself. "Yes, certainly. Please do not think me unhospita . . . that is, ungrateful for your assistance. I fear I have simply not had time to think . . ."

He rose just as the butler returned to inquire if any refreshments were required, Mr. Melville having neglected to ring for any. Melville, still distracted, requested the man to bring tea and sherry to the drawing room in ten minutes. Antonia observed him during this little scene and decided that, on the whole, his behavior was too much that of a worried parent to lead her to believe that he had had any previous knowledge of Elena's disappearance or was in any way responsible for it. She did not know why she still could not warm to him.

They proceeded silently up the stairs, all—except her husband, Antonia guessed—slightly uncomfortable with this peculiar exercise. Antonia hesitated for a moment in the doorway to Miss Melville's room, reluctant to intrude into such a private domain, but her husband apparently had no such scruples. He touched nothing, but his eyes took in everything. She could not tell if he saw anything of interest, but hoped he would tell her later if he did.

She herself noted nothing unusual. It was a pleasant, airy room, feminine but almost impersonal, as if Elena hid her private self away behind cupboard doors or inside drawers—or she had an inordinately conscientious maid.

The only discordant note in the immaculate room was struck by a crumpled ball of paper on the floor beside a wastepaper basket. While her husband began opening drawers, Antonia leaned over to pick it up. Then she noticed more like it in the basket. She extracted several of them, then opened one, and another. They all began the same way, some going on for several lines, others stopping abruptly after only a few words.

My dearest Carey,

Once again I must seek your forgiveness and beg you, if you can, to forget. Should you be unable to forget me, for I shall never forget you, it would be my greatest happiness to think we might begin anew . . .

Antonia tore her eyes from the page and tossed the crumpled sheets back into the basket. She knew it! She had been certain that Elena still loved Carey, and here was the proof! Elena must have been attempting to put her feelings in words—could she have succeeded and sent a final clean copy to Carey before she went away, perhaps telling him where she had gone?

She slipped one of the rejected letters into her pocket. If

Carey had not received a letter, she would show him the draft, and beg Elena's forgiveness later for her interference. But not to do anything would be worse than doing the wrong thing.

"Are any of her clothes missing?" Kedrington asked. Melville opened a wardrobe and said he thought there might be, but he could not tell. Antonia looked over his shoulder into a neat row of dresses hanging from pegs and hats lined up militarily on a shelf above them, and decided that at least the walking dress Elena had worn when they last met in the park was missing.

"Perhaps . . ." she began. Both gentlemen looked to her, as if only another female could learn anything from an apparently—to their eyes—undisturbed feminine sanctuary.

"Perhaps she has only gone away to think."

"To think?" Melville inquired, mystified.

"About the future," Antonia supplied. "About her betrothal to Carey. Perhaps she has had second thoughts and is unsure how to approach him again."

There was a silence as the gentlemen attempted to understand this. "But *where* might she have gone?" Kedrington asked, "to . . . er, think."

"That is a puzzle," Melville conceded.

"Has she no acquaintances in the country—or even another part of London?" Antonia inquired.

Melville shrugged helplessly, apparently forgetting the fictitious sister he had employed before when Elena did not wish to receive them. Antonia had not forgotten, and this confirmed her opinion that Melville was truly concerned about his ward.

"She may have friends I have not met," he said, "but . . . perhaps I should call in the Runners after all."

"No, don't do that," Kedrington said. "Let me make a few discreet inquiries first. We would not want to broadcast her disappearance any sooner than necessary, would we?"

"No, no, of course not."

Melville appeared somewhat relieved at this offer and recovered some of his more usual dignity. He escorted his visitors back to the parlor and engaged them in only slightly stilted conversation over refreshments for a quarter of an hour until Antonia decided it was past time for a polite departure. Her husband appeared lost in thought, so there was no telling when he would think to say his farewells.

"Well?" Antonia demanded when they had returned home and were once again comfortably situated in his lordship's study. "What do you think has happened?"

"Something unexpected—to Melville, at least."

"That much was obvious," Antonia objected. "Do you want to know what I think?"

"I am all agog."

"I think that Elena has been kidnapped by whoever is behind this plot to steal the marbles in order to blackmail Dimitri into doing something for them that he does not wish to do."

He thought about this. "Very interesting."

"Thank you."

"But indistinct. What 'something,' for example?"

"Taking the blame for the theft?"

"If he is indeed involved in it, I should think taking the sole responsibility would be a prize of the highest order. He would gain the support of the anti-Elgin faction and become a hero in his homeland."

"Oh. Well, suppose he *was* involved, and has changed his mind—being an honorable man at heart—and he is being blackmailed into continuing to take part."

"You have taken quite a fancy to blackmail. And who do you see as being behind this plot?" he asked, getting back to the point.

"Oh, dear. I was afraid you would ask me that. There are so many possibilities—most of which you have been so disobliging as to point out—that I cannot make up my mind."

"And what has happened to your theory that she has simply gone away by herself to think about the future?"

"That remains my belief on the grounds of its being the simplest. However, as we discussed before, one must consider all the possibilities."

He made no reply to that, and Antonia could see him almost visibly turn his mind to some other subject. When he made no further observations, however, she asked, "What are you thinking now?"

He smiled. "About how this room has become the equivalent of the Duke's tent during the war, or any meeting room at the foreign office where strategy is planned."

"But we have not come up with any plan, much less any strategy."

"That comes after we consider all the possibilities."

"And you have always said you did not wish to enter political life yourself. It appears you have a knack for it after all."

"As do you, my love."

"Perhaps, but the nation would never be so sensible as to allow females into elected office."

The possibilities to which this topic might have led were left unexplored when Trotter knocked on the door. Bidden to enter, he handed his lordship a letter.

"By the by, Trotter," Antonia said, "has there been any message lately for my brother?"

"No, my lady."

"Oh. Well, thank you, Trotter."

When the butler had departed, Kedrington opened the note.

"It is from Carey," he said.

"Do not tell me he has found Elena!"

"No, but he has found her trail. This letter was sent from Croydon. He has been inquiring at all the posting inns going south, and had a bit of luck when an ostler remembered Miss Melville from his description. Apparently she was traveling alone."

"Well, that is good news," Antonia said. After a moment, however, when Kedrington made no comment, she said, "It is good news, isn't it? Carey will not have to face a kidnapper and Elena will explain everything to him when he catches up to her."

"You're right, of course."

"And," Antonia went on, a happy thought striking her, "they will have a little time alone to talk and to settle their differences. I'm sure they will come back to us reconciled and we can announced their betrothal after all."

"I'm sure you're right again, my love."

Chapter 19

∽

The day after Carey Fairfax left London in pursuit of his bride, Lord Kedrington left his own wife at home, anxiously awaiting further news from her brother, and took himself to the Strand. His object was a club known as the Socratic Society, which he knew to be patronized by Greek expatriates. The building that housed it was situated in a little lane off the Strand and had begun life as a coffeehouse. It had been a hotel when the Society took it over, and a little of both previous incarnations lingered into the present one. In recent years, it had become known as a hotbed of Greek nationalism, and it was said by some that the coming war for independence from Greece's Turkish rulers would be launched from there.

Kedrington had been introduced to the club by Lord Byron the year before the poet's departure from the London literary and social scene. Kedrington reflected wryly that if any English artist, however brilliant the light he had previously cast, removed himself from his setting, it was as if he had never existed. The notion that Byron could be thriving and producing his best work somewhere other than in his native land was as foreign to many so-called patrons of the arts as Greece itself. His works were still sold and read, of course, but as those of a foreign artist.

Kedrington entered the small, unmarked building that housed the Socratic Society and handed his hat to the porter. "Good afternoon, Kostis."

"Good afternoon, my lord," the porter replied, gratified to be remembered. "We have not seen you for some time."

"Do not reproach me for it, Kostis. I confess I have become lazy, lulled into stupor by the rich food and drink to be had in the St. James's clubs."

"We will enliven your spirit here, sir, not dull your senses."

Kedrington grinned. "Is anyone about whom I may know?"

"Do make yourself comfortable in the sitting room, my lord, and I will bring you a coffee. There are very few members here at present, but more will be arriving for dinner shortly."

Kedrington followed this advice and made himself comfortable in a corner of the room where he would not immediately be seen by anyone entering through the only door. The only other occupants of the place were three young men, students by the look of them, poring over a Greek newspaper and speaking in low but intense tones among themselves as a pall of tobacco smoke rose above them.

The porter came in with the promised coffee, and Kedrington thanked him. He sipped at the thick, sweet brew, then picked up a copy of the *Examiner* and prepared to wait.

He was shortly rewarded when Dimitri Metaxis strode into the room and joined the group around the table in the opposite corner. He did not immediately notice the other occupant of the room, which gave Kedrington a chance to study him.

He was a handsome young man, his features stronger, masculine variations on Elena Melville's exotic good looks. He was dressed respectably, but neither in the first stare of fashion nor the newest of apparel. On closer inspection, his cuffs would doubtless prove to be frayed. His hair was in disarray, probably from his walk here, and after cursorily running his hand over it he paid no more attention to his appearance. He looked like a man who had weightier matters

on his mind than the cut of his coat or the length of his hair.
Doubtless he did.

He did not, however, look like a desperate man, Kedrington reflected—at any rate, no more so than any young man
with more energy than physical releases for it. Carey had
been that way when he first went to Spain and had picked
up the behavior again on his return to England, where spar-
ring sessions at Jackson's and curricle races were tame
sport compared to being shot at by French artillery.

Nor did Dimitri look like a natural plotter. His countenance was too open, and his manner, judging by the anima-
tion of his gestures, too expressive to lead anyone to
suppose he had any talent for prevarication. Kedrington decided that the time had come to put this theory to a test.

He put his coffee cup down with an audible clatter and
rustled his paper. Dimitri immediately turned around,
blanched when he recognized Kedrington, and bolted for
the door. The viscount, quicker on his feet, was there before him.

"I should like a word," he said.

"I have nothing to say to you!" Dimitri responded an-
grily, attempting to pull his arm out of Kedrington's grip.

"Nonsense," Kedrington said mildly, steering the young
man toward the chair he himself had recently occupied.
"We are members of the same club, both here to pass a
restful hour in congenial company. Surely, we must have
other . . . er, interests in common?"

He pushed Dimitri lightly but firmly into the chair, and
pulled up another close to him. He sat in it, effectively
blocking Dimitri's path to the door.

"Would you care for a glass of wine?" Kedrington asked
amiably. "As I recall, they have quite a respectable retsina
here. Indeed, this is the only club in London that does, so
far as I am aware."

Dimitri looked as if he would refuse, but then shrugged
and appeared to give up any further attempt at resistance.
He crossed his legs and assumed a nonchalant pose.

"Why not."

A waiter appeared before Dimitri was aware of his being summoned, and took their order. Kedrington smiled inwardly, amused at the expression on his young guest's face. No, he was decidedly not cut out to be a plotter.

"I expect you are wondering how I was able to summon that waiter so quickly," Kedrington said, adopting the tone Brummel had used when he deigned to pass on one of his secrets of the toilette. "Possibly he has not responded to even your most vociferous demands with such alacrity in the past. I could change that for you if I wished."

"It is only because you are an earl and he is a toadeater," Dimitri said sneering.

"A mere viscount. Nonetheless, the principle is the same. Rank does have its privileges. Yet, even when one is a mere viscount, one may be treated like a duke if one takes the time and thought to pave the way ahead."

The wine arrived and Kedrington told the waiter to leave the bottle. He handed the man a coin with more ostentation than he would normally employ, and the waiter bowed himself out with effusive thanks. Dimitri scowled at the exhibition. At least, thought Kedrington, he was not unobservant. But would he learn the lesson?

"Wealth, of course, speeds a man along that path, and the ride is always more comfortable in a well-sprung vehicle."

Dimitri drained his glass in three quick swallows and refilled it.

"You may have that bottle," Kedrington said.

"What is your point?" Dimitri asked, feigning an indifference to the answer, which Kedrington suspected he did not feel.

"First," he said, "that one of the privileges of rank and wealth is that one enjoys the freedom to spend one's riches where one pleases. Too many wealthy men, admittedly, spend it solely on themselves and their own pleasures. I am not one of them. I will listen to any appeal for funds on behalf of someone less fortunate than myself or for the purpose of enriching the cultural life of this nation. Or any nation."

This, he saw, had focused Dimitri's interest.

"Or," he continued, "for any worthy cause, either cultural or social, or even political."

He paused, waiting for a response. Dimitri said nothing until the pause had lengthened appreciably. Then, growing restive, he gave in.

"I'm not sure if you are threatening me or offering your support," he admitted with a wry smile. The smile lit his face and seemed to make his eyes shine. Kedrington thought it was a pity that young Mr. Metaxis seemed to have no time or taste for the society his sister had adopted. He could have his pick of beautiful heiresses.

"The choice is yours."

"What do you want from me?"

"Who has kidnapped your sister?"

The suddenness of this obviously unexpected question caught Dimitri by surprise, and Kedrington was sure by the expression on his face that he knew nothing about any kidnapping plot.

"You're mad. Elena hasn't been kidnapped."

"Then where is she?"

"Safe at home, I would imagine," Dimitri replied, retreating from his candidness—although not so far that Kedrington's earlier effort to gain it was entirely wasted. "Why don't you badger that guardian of hers? I wouldn't put it past him to lock her in a cellar."

"She disappeared from London the same day you did."

"I didn't disappear. I only moved out of that hotel." He grimaced. "It got so that every time I went out the door, someone followed me. God knows where they thought I would lead them. I wanted to get rid of them, that's all. As you can plainly see, I haven't disappeared."

"But Elena has. What do you know about it?"

Dimitri rose, banging his glass on the table. "I don't know. I don't care. Elena has disowned her family—why should I care what happens to her?"

"She hasn't disowned you."

Dimitri picked up the bottle and slammed the cork back

into it. "Thank you for your hospitality, my lord, but I have an appointment and cannot continue this amiable conversation at this time. Good day."

He rose and made for the door.

"One moment." Kedrington's voice was soft yet steely enough to stop Dimitri in his tracks. He turned back. Kedrington had remained seated.

"You haven't heard my proposition."

Dimitri hesitated, curiosity warring with suspicion, but finally he turned back and sat down again at Kedrington's table, this time at an openly hostile angle.

"Well, what is it?"

"What is your connection with this plot to steal the Parthenon marbles?"

This question appeared to so startle the younger man that he became affixed to his seat, unable to rise and make another dramatic exit.

"What do you know about it?" he asked at last, leaning forward to speak in a low but forceful whisper.

"A good deal. I shan't bore you with the details just yet, but I can tell you that the thieves will be captured soon, perhaps even tonight."

"How?" Dimitri asked eagerly. He had cast off the last vestiges of his indifferent pose, Kedrington noted with satisfaction.

"I shall reveal that later as well. What I want to know now—what I am proposing to you—is that you help me and my friends to accomplish this."

"Why should I? If you think I'm involved, I wonder that you are willing to take me into your confidence."

"I never accused you of being involved."

"Perhaps not here, today. But I am beginning to suspect you set those men to following me. What is your interest in the affair?"

Kedrington smiled wryly. "Again, too long a tale to embark on here. If you help us, you know, any remaining suspicion attached to you can be dashed."

"What do I care if I am suspected? No one can prove anything."

"My dear boy, what touching faith you have in the British legal system. And you coming from a possession of the Ottoman empire."

"Greece is not Ottoman!" Dimitri hissed, leaping onto a different high horse. "It will be independent in my lifetime—in my youth—I swear it!"

Kedrington raised a hand as if to ward off a blow. "Do not harangue me, sir. You will not move me from my position."

"I do not know what your position is."

"I thought we discussed that. I am in a position to assist you materially as well as legally if you agree to my proposal. What say you?"

Dimitri hesitated, and Kedrington could almost see the wheels of his mind turning as he pondered the possibilities.

"When do I start?"

"Now. Tonight. Give me your word that you will meet me at a place I will appoint, and I will take it. Or you may come with me now, and I will tell you all those long tales on the way."

"Will you give me dinner if I do?"

Kedrington held out his hand. Dimitri shook it.

"We have a bargain."

Pausing on the way out only to write a note to Antonia and give it to the ever-helpful Kostis to have delivered, Kedrington escorted Dimitri down the lane toward the Strand, whither Kostis had hastened to summon a hack for them.

Chapter 20

~

Sometime in the hours before dawn the following morning, Lady Kedrington herself, holding a candle in one hand and clutching a Chinese-patterned silk robe to her breast with the other, opened the door to her husband.

"Duncan, where have you been? I have been breathless with anticipation! When I received your note—oh, good heavens! It *is* Mr. Metaxis, is it not?"

Her husband gently moved her aside so that he could enter his own house. She aimed a kick at his shin, but as she had neglected to put on her slippers, the effect was less than wounding.

"I do beg your pardon, sir," she said, addressing Dimitri again with a formality that warred with her attire. "Duncan neglected to mention that he would bring you directly . . . that is, I am glad to see you."

Mr. Metaxis was trying very hard not to look at Lady Kedrington, and even in the near-darkness, her husband was amused to see that he was blushing furiously at being subjected to her state of dishabille. Antonia herself became aware of this after what seemed a very long and awkward moment and exclaimed, inadequately, "Oh, dear."

"I have invited Mr. Metaxis to spend the night—or what is left of it—with us. Go upstairs, my love, while I rouse Trotter to find our guest a bed. Then I will join you and re-count our exploits of the evening."

"What exploits?"

"The evil ones have been vanquished and the lost found. In other words, we caught the thieves and the marbles are being returned to their proper place—or at least their current residence—as we speak."

"Oh, no!" Antonia gasped, as if he had announced that the house was on fire.

Even Dimitri stared at this reaction. Kedrington looked put out that his news had met with such an unexpected reaction and said, "I had hoped to please my lady with my valiant deeds—even if I did take all the credit undeservedly. May I inquire what has upset that expectation?"

"But I have news as well," Antonia said. "I have found out who owns the building above the passage—the one I entered by that night."

Despite her eagerness to impart her news, she paused for dramatic effect at this juncture, and Mr. Metaxis, who had thus far been silent, demanded, "Who?"

"Arthur Melville."

This silenced both gentlemen temporarily. Then Kedrington, realizing the implications, said, "Good God."

"Precisely so," said his lady.

"He owns the cellar in which we found the missing marbles?" Dimitri asked, still not quite comprehending her meaning. Antonia nodded.

"Then he is involved in the plot!" Dimitri exclaimed. "I never liked the man, and now I know why!"

"Indeed," Antonia said, "I have been thinking about it—while waiting all this time for you to come home, dearest—and I believe he must be the mastermind behind the plot."

Kedrington was thoughtful. "Perhaps—or perhaps only the organizer, an intermediary. Surely, he hasn't the money to support—"

Dimitri interrupted. "Whatever his involvement, if he hears about the gang being captured, he will flee!"

Kedrington looked at him. "You're right. We must reach him before he hears the news—or go after him if he has already done so. One of the gang would no doubt give him up sooner or later, and he would realize that."

"Wait for me. I'm going with you."

"Antonia—"

"Do not forbid me, Duncan. If you do, I will only follow you."

Kedrington sighed as his wife's figure disappeared up the stairs. Then he turned to Dimitri. "She would, you know."

"Let me go ahead," Dimitri said. "Perhaps I could detain him."

"No, I don't want to chance your being caught alone with him. If I am with you every moment, I will be able to swear to your movements tonight—should it come to that."

He lighted the candle placed on a small table near the door and showed Dimitri into the sitting room. He scribbled a hasty letter, summoned a footman, and sent him with the letter off to Bow Street. He then roused a groom and had a phaeton readied, as well as a horse for Dimitri.

By this time, Antonia had reappeared, hastily but practically dressed in a dark green riding habit, boots, and a veiled hat. She was pulling on her gloves as she descended the stairs and said, "Betty was none too pleased at being awakened an hour earlier than necessary, but I told her she could go back to sleep for another two if she liked. Are we ready?"

It was not yet dawn when the trio set out. Only a faint flush of light appeared over the rooftops to their right as they crossed Oxford Street and proceeded past Portland Square toward Gloucester Place. It was very little time before they reached the Melville residence, and Kedrington pulled his horses to a stop on the opposite side of the street. The groom jumped down from the rear of the phaeton to take their heads as Antonia looked up. There was a light in an upper window, but no sign of activity in the rest of the house or outside it.

"He is still here!" Antonia exclaimed.

"Thank God Elena is not," Dimitri said, pulling his horse alongside.

"The Runners do not seem to have arrived yet," Kedrington said, glancing around. "We had best wait here."

"But there is a door on the other side of the house," Dimitri said. "It lets into a garden that has a gate into the mews and thence provides an egress to Baker Street. He could get out that way!"

Antonia glanced at Dimitri, wondering briefly how he could be so intimately acquainted with the house if his sister's guardian had forbidden it to him and there was such mutual dislike between the two men.

She dismissed her doubts, however, when Kedrington said, "Very well. Dimitri, you find your way to that door and watch it. If Melville leaves that way, follow and leave a trail. On no account attack him or let him see you. Do you think you can restrain yourself long enough to do that?"

"Yes, of course, but . . ." Dimitri had apparently been visited by the same doubts that Antonia had experienced. "But . . . ?"

"How can you trust me not to run away again—or to help Melville?"

Kedrington looked at him, then smiled. "I shall leave you, while you are waiting at the door, to ponder the possible consequences of either of those actions on your part— and any reasons I may have to trust or distrust you. Now, go!"

Dimitri wasted no time in carrying out his orders. They watched as he carefully unlocked the gate to the square near the house and made his way silently around the back of the house.

"Where did he get the key to that gate?" Antonia wondered.

"I suspect he has been seeing his sister on the sly."

She turned to stare at him. "You mean, it was all a hum about their being estranged?"

"So it would seem. I daresay he will tell us about it when all this is over."

"You had better tell me all about catching that gang *now*," Antonia said, folding her arms across her chest and glaring at him.

"I regret that you will have to wait at least a little longer," he said. "Do you see that chimney sweep?"

A tall man in black, carrying a broom over one shoulder, was strolling down the street toward them.

"He's rather large for a chimney sweep," she remarked.

"Very observant. He's a Runner. Doubtless there are others about. Which means it is time for us to pay a call."

He got down from his perch and walked around to her side of the vehicle. It occurred to Antonia that if they waited where they were, Melville would walk out his door and into the arms of the Runners. But a moment later, it also occurred to her that once he left his house, it would be that much easier for him to get away, and if he should go out the back way, only Dimitri would be there to intercept him.

She put her hand out to her husband, who helped her down to the pavement, then took her arm. They walked across the street and up to the house like any couple paying a conventional call at a more usual hour of the day. But when they reached the door, Kedrington said, "One moment."

He pulled a key out of his pocket and tried it in the door, but it did not fit. He shrugged.

"What *are* you doing?"

"Never mind. I didn't really think it would fit, but there are all those possibilities."

"What can you mean?"

He grinned and said, "Later." Then he raised the knocker and flattened himself against the side of the entrance where he would not immediately be seen by whoever opened the door. Antonia understood what he wanted and prepared herself.

But it was only a sleepy butler who eventually answered their knock. Antonia recomposed her features again and said firmly, "Good morning. I am sorry to disturb you at this hour, but it is imperative that I speak with Mr. Melville. I have distressing news about his ward, which must be conveyed to him at once."

As she spoke, she moved into the hallway, unopposed by the bemused butler, who said nothing until Kedrington slipped in beside her and made for the stairs.

"'Ere!" he shouted, sufficiently awake now to be alarmed but not to remember his dignity. "You can't go up there!"

"He can go anywhere he likes," Antonia said in an affable tone, as if remarking on the antics of a precocious child. "And if you wish to keep your post when Miss Melville returns—for when she does, she will be mistress of this house—I suggest that you remove yourself at once."

The butler stared at her, glanced once more in the direction Kedrington had taken, and then turned and did as he was told, disappearing into the nether regions of the house.

A moment later, sounds of an altercation could be heard from the upper floor. Antonia bit her lip, telling herself that Duncan was more than capable of defending himself, yet trying to decide if she could help in any way. But then there was another knock on the door.

She opened it. On the step was the chimney sweep, accompanied by a burly-looking person in a porkpie hat.

"Lady Kedrington?" said the sweep, politely raising his black hat. "May we come in?"

"Please do," she said. The two men bowed, stepped around her, and made for the stairs as well.

"This is absurd," she muttered to herself. "I may as well be at the pantomime."

Loud footsteps sounded on the floor above, and Arthur Melville himself appeared at the top of the stairs, carrying a portmanteau and pursued at a less frantic pace by Kedrington, who appeared to be flushing his bird rather than intending to bring it down.

Melville spotted Antonia a moment before he saw the Runners blocking his escape. She smiled sweetly and raised her hand in a little wave just as the other two men clasped

Melville firmly on each side and hauled him toward the outer door. Antonia opened it again and stepped aside. Melville glared at her, his former avuncular expression gone.

"This is your doing!" he accused her.

"*My* doing?" Antonia queried, all innocence. "No, my dear sir, it is all *your* doing."

"Why is it that criminals always place the blame for their misdeeds on someone else?" Kedrington asked his wife in a tone of disinterested inquiry. "What is more astounding is that they actually believe they are the injured party."

He turned on Melville then, his smile gone. "And what is certain is that only *petty* criminals like you, Melville, invariably behave like that. The real masters of the game are eager to take the credit. Who's behind this, Melville? Who's paying you?"

"You'll never know," Melville said, sneering.

"It will go easier for you if you tell us the whole story."

"That's what you think," Melville said. Antonia thought she saw a spark of fear in his eyes that had nothing to do with her husband's threats. It must be true then, that Arthur Melville was not the instigator of the plot to steal the marbles. But whom could he be shielding?

"What have you done with Elena?" she asked him suddenly, hoping to catch him off guard.

He hesitated for a moment, and the two men holding him began dragging him out the door.

"Wait!" Antonia cried.

Melville looked at her. His expression was no longer readable. He had succeeded in shutting himself away from the world, as he would be shut away physically now.

He said, "I don't know where she is."

He muttered a curse as the men renewed their grip and he was dragged out the door, none too gently. Antonia raised her eyebrows.

"What a rude man."

Kedrington came up to her, brushing imaginary dust from his sleeves. He looked as if he had just dressed for the day, rather than spent the night, as well as the last few min-. utes, chasing miscreants.

"I wish I could stay as impeccably groomed for even one hour as you do for an entire day," Antonia told him enviously. "How do you do it?"

"It is all in the movement," he said.

"What do you mean?"

"I am economical in mine. You are extravagant. Clothes cannot lie quietly on you, and they show their agitation in wrinkles."

"I never heard such nonsense. Where are they taking him?"

"Bow Street Magistrates' Court, I trust. They will waste no time prosecuting him if I have anything to say about it."

They stepped outside, and Kedrington closed the door behind them. They watched Melville, still cursing, being bundled into a closed carriage and driven away.

Antonia gasped. "Duncan, we didn't make him tell us where Elena is!"

"He really doesn't know," said a third voice.

"Mr. Metaxis! What can you mean?"

Dimitri had joined them as Melville was being led off. He said, "He doesn't know, because it was I who took Elena away."

Chapter 21

Antonia stared at Dimitri. "But why? I mean, I suppose I know why—to keep her away from Melville?"

Dimitri nodded. "It was not that he mistreated her in any way, but I feared that if things went wrong—as they did for Melville tonight—she might come to harm."

"But—"

"It is another long story, I'm afraid," Kedrington interrupted. "But she is safe for now."

"In that case, we had better go home so you can start telling me all about it."

"I trust you won't mind if I sleep off all this excitement first," he said with an exaggerated yawn.

"Why, Duncan, I thought you went through the entire war without sleep. Carey is always saying so."

"Carey is a liar. Besides, I am older now."

"How very disappointing."

He looked at her as they seated themselves once more within their carriage. "What, my being older or Carey being a prevaricator?"

Dimitri, seating himself opposite them, smiled at this nonsense. "I am beginning to understand why my sister fell in love with your brother, Lady Kedrington."

"Why?" she asked, genuinely curious.

"Our family was a happy one, too, when we were children. There was always a great deal of laughter and joking, even though our circumstances were straitened. We were taken away from that at an early age, however, and thereafter Elena at least was much hedged about with restrictions and British notions of proper behavior. The first time I met her after I came to this country, I thought she had forgotten how to laugh."

He paused, looking out the carriage window into a past that was beyond Antonia's vision.

Antonia reached her hand out to clasp his warmly. "I hope you will confide in us when all this is over, Dimitri. We should very much like to see you, as well as your sister, become part of the family."

He looked at her, and she thought she saw a great longing in his expression. But he only smiled and said, "Thank you."

It was full daylight before Lord and Lady Kedrington finally retired to their beds, where they slept soundly for four hours. At ten o'clock, Antonia, wakened by the questions knocking at the back of her mind demanding to be answered, rang for coffee and entered her husband's bedroom. He was still in bed, but not sleeping; he lay with one arm flung above his head, his head resting on his hand and his eyes open.

"Oh, Duncan, I'm so glad you're awake." She climbed into the bed beside him and propped herself up with one of his pillows.

"You were able to sleep for a few hours, I hope?" she asked with concern, as he sat up also.

"Never fear, my love. I slept the sleep of the righteous."

"Don't be smug. You have done a good deed today—or I suppose it was last night—but do not let it lull you into self-satisfaction."

He smiled. "I have no doubt you will bring me back down to earth should I take myself too seriously."

The breakfast tray arrived, and they both drank a cup of coffee. Antonia nibbled on a slice of toast and said, "Now tell me the story."

"I thought bedtime stories were for before one went to sleep. Which one would you like to hear?"

"How you caught the gang."

"Ah, that was not so difficult. It required only the good luck of finding that passage and then a little patience. We—Robin Campbell and I, that is—scheduled the watch so that it would appear from the outside that it had been reduced, in order not to alarm the thieves with an extra contingent of guards. They were there, of course, but not visible. Robin even contrived to fall asleep at his post once or twice."

"By the way, what is Robin going to do after the marbles are finally installed in Montagu House?"

"Do?"

"For occupation. Will he be asked to stay on at the museum, given his heroic assistance in catching the thieves?"

He looked at her sternly. "That must not be made public, Antonia."

"Why not?"

"It could embarrass the government."

"Oh, pooh. The government embarrasses itself every time one of its members opens his mouth."

He laughed. "Well, then, consider the embarrassment—not to mention possible legal difficulties—to Robin and all those involved, including Dimitri, who might be accused of concealing the plot or the plotters and thus unnecessarily endangering a national treasure."

"Could that happen?"

"Who knows? Anything is possible."

She frowned. "Oh, very well. But your Aunt Julia will worm the story out of one of us, see if she doesn't."

He chuckled. "Well, Julia is at least discreet. She will keep it from Hester and thus from the world."

"But you will help Robin, won't you, if he needs it?"

"Of course. He does not accept charity gracefully, but I shall do what I can."

"And I shall invite him to some of our parties and introduce him to some eligible young ladies."

Kedrington flung his arm over his eyes as if to ward off some frightening vision. "Heaven spare us."

"Why shouldn't he want to settle down with some nice girl—especially if she has a little money of her own?"

He said nothing more, and she began beating him with a pillow. For a few moments there was some danger of chaos as the coffeepot teetered on the trembling bedside table, until Antonia tossed the pillow at her feet and sighed.

"You have distracted me from your story," she accused him. "Go on with it."

Still chuckling, he rearranged himself and said, "Where was I?"

"Robin was falling asleep at his post."

"Oh, yes. We apparently succeeded in lulling the thieves into believing that there was no suspicion of a theft and that the fakes had not been noticed. Last night, they struck again. There were four of them, but five of us, counting Dimitri, who was an unexpected bonus. One of our men heard the thieves in the passageway—where he was hidden behind that row of support beams you may remember, and after they had passed by him, he went out the door you entered through and came around to warn us.

"We waited until they had actually loaded another piece on a cart and were hauling it toward the passage entrance, then surprised them. They were outnumbered, and we were armed. They offered no resistance."

Antonia doubted the strict accuracy of this statement, having noticed a bruise on Dimitri's cheek, but she did not inquire more closely into it. Everyone was safe now, she told herself; nothing else mattered.

"What were they going to do with the sculptures?"

"They were hired thugs with no loyalty to their employer, so they knew very little. They had been paid only to take the pieces, conceal them in crates, and hide them in that cellar where we saw them. Robin and his friends returned them the same way and put the fakes in their place for use as evidence, should it come to that. May I have another cup of coffee now? All this storytelling is making me thirsty."

She obligingly poured him another cup. "How did Dimitri come to be there?" she asked.

He told her how he had met Dimitri at the Socratic Society and had persuaded him to assist.

"So he had been involved with the plot originally? Why did he break with the gang?"

"He found out they were doing it only for the money and had no interest in returning the marbles to Greece. After that, he pretended to go along—he was originally recruited to oversee the construction of the fakes, which it seems were done in all innocence by a student at the Royal Academy. Dimitri suspected Melville and was watching him to see if he might give himself away somehow. He was becoming frustrated about his inability to do anything and because everyone—including you, my love—seemed to be following his every movement. I was not a moment too soon in reaching him, and he fell in with my suggestion that he assist us because he was at a dead end himself."

He put his cup down and looked at her. "Now it is time for you to tell a story, my love. How did you find out that Arthur Melville was involved? I had just learned it from Dimitri that same day."

"How did he know?"

"He overheard a conversation between Melville and one of the thugs one day when he came into the house secretly to see his sister. He was unsure of the meaning of what he heard at first, since he had never actually met the man who organized the thefts, but when he found himself being followed, he suspected Melville and so began making his own inquiries."

Antonia wrapped her arms around her knees and put her chin on them for a moment as she considered all this.

"Now your story," Kedrington said.

Antonia smiled. "Actually, I have two stories to tell you, but as to Arthur Melville—well, you know I never trusted him."

"You gave no indication of it."

"Well, I hope I am civil to everyone unless they prove themselves unworthy of civility."

"But he had not, until last night."

"Please do not cavil, Duncan. You are distracting me from my story."

"I beg your pardon. Do go on."

"Well, I got to thinking about that house on Cork Street, where the stolen marbles were taken. I had noticed it particularly when I was following Dimitri and Carey from Grillon's Hotel—"

"Kindly do not remind me of that folly."

"But it is part of the story!"

"Very well, go on."

"The house was unoccupied, which did not seem peculiar at the time, since I was looking for Carey—who tells me he simply walked through the yard to the mews and then to Bond Street and never noticed the door I went into."

"He was not looking for secret passages."

"Do not make excuses for him, Duncan. Anyway, that house did not have a number, so I made a note of the numbers on either side of it and later sent Milford to the property office to inquire about their owners."

"Milford! You purloined my valet to run your errands?"

"Well, you reminded me just recently that he had been in Spain with you. I thought that some of your expertise in these matters might have rubbed off. Besides, he can speak and act like a gentleman, so I knew he would not be turned away, even if he did not mention your name."

"I must have a chat with Milford about his extracurricular activities. If he doesn't have enough work here to keep him occupied, perhaps I should find some more."

"Don't be absurd. You know you want him at your beck and call, even when you don't need him. Besides, you had not been home all day, had you?"

"Never mind that. So you found out that Melville owned one of those houses?"

"Yes, and then I remembered his mentioning, that first

day when we met him at Burlington House, that he had property in the neighborhood, so I put two and two together."

"And came up with three."

"What do you mean?"

"I mean, we still do not know who financed the plot, and if we do not discover the answer soon, he may slip out of our reach."

"Have you no suspicion?"

"Suspicion, yes. But one needs proof."

She sat up, saying eagerly, "Whom do you suspect?"

Before he could answer, however, there was a rap on the door. Kedrington got out of bed, opened the door a crack, and turned back with a letter in his hand.

"It's from Carey," he said. "He is in Lewes and says he believes he knows where Elena is and is going to rescue her. Curse it—we should have sent someone to stop him when we learned that Elena is safe."

"We can still send Dimitri."

"Yes, I shall do so at once." But he continued reading the letter, then exclaimed, "Oh, my God."

"What?" Alarmed, Antonia jumped out of bed and snatched the letter from her husband's fingers. It had been posted from the White Hart in Lewes the night before. She scanned it, saw nothing alarming, and said, "What is the matter, Duncan?"

But he had already pulled the bell to summon Milford and was preparing to dress for the day.

"My love, call someone to wake Dimitri, quickly. He must come with me."

"But where to?"

"Sussex. I believe I do know who is behind the plot— and Elena may be in danger after all."

Chapter 22

~

Carey Fairfax woke to the thunder of battering rams at his gates. He sat up, groaned, and looked around him. Oh, yes, he remembered now. He was in Sussex, at some inn or other, and he had come to rescue Elena from her imprisonment in . . . where was it again?

The pounding on his door continued, and Carey realized belatedly that it was only a knock, probably the waiter with his breakfast. What time was it? He stumbled to his feet, pushed the window curtain aside, and blinked at the daylight that shone in his eyes. Then—with some effort, for he felt oddly weak—he pulled the door open.

"What time is it?" he demanded of the startled waiter. "What's the name of this town?"

"Lewes, sir, and it's goin' on eleven, sir. We couldn't wake you earlier. You all right, sir?"

Carey groaned and held his head between his hands. He could not possibly have imbibed all that much wine last night. No—he remembered now—he had drunk only two tankards of ale. Why did his head ache so?

He waved feebly toward the single table in the room. "Put the tray down there."

The waiter did so, and backed off, eyeing Carey suspiciously. "Tankard of ale, sir? Hair of the dog, mayhap?"

Carey fumbled in his pocket for a coin.

"No, thanks. I'll be all right in a trice."

"Very well, sir," said the waiter, accepting the coin and bowing himself out.

Carey sat down with a thud and closed his eyes. That made his head ache even more. He opened them and poured himself some coffee, then dug into the eggs and bacon the waiter had brought, scarcely tasting them.

After he had eaten, however, he began to feel better. At least his head was no longer pounding.

What in heaven's name had he drunk last night?

As his head began to clear, the events of the previous night came into sharper focus. He had vaguely remembered Elena saying something about a relation living in Sussex, so for lack of any other plan, he had taken the road south from London. Thorough questioning of the ostlers at every stage stop along the way had yielded results at Croydon. Fortunately, Elena was easily distinguishable from most young English ladies by her coloring, and once he had found out what sort of conveyance she was traveling in, the task was easier. She was being driven by a servant and accompanied by a maid, and the party seemed to be in no hurry to reach their destination.

This last struck Carey as decidedly peculiar, but he did not allow himself to relax his own pace because of it. He failed to find anyone remembering Elena after Cuckfield, however, and was delayed for hours, inquiring at every hostelry near the inn where they had left the carriage and horses to—and that was another very odd thing—wander about the town like any set of gawking sightseers! What was there to be seen in Cuckfield anyway? They had even stopped for dinner, taken at leisure in a well-known hotel, before setting off again, as he at last discovered, in the direction of Lewes.

By the time Carey arrived at Lewes, however, it was dark, and while he contemplated this as a factor in his favor, it took him additional hours to identify the house where he thought Elena must be held, by which time he was exhausted.

Since the house was some distance outside the town, and

since Elena did not appear to be in any immediate danger, he elected to spend the night at the White Hart. In the morning, he would simply approach the house on some pretext, ascertain how closely Elena might be guarded, and take her away by either stealth or force of arms. He would have preferred the latter, being eager to prove his valor to his lady love, but even Carey recognized that such a course might end in disaster. He would take the night to think about it.

After obtaining a room, he had entered the taproom of the inn for a nightcap. Sitting alone with his ale, he had glanced around the room, hoping for company. He was not a solitary drinker, and a little conversation to take his mind off his worry over Elena would be welcome.

He spotted a vaguely familiar face at a corner table and approached it.

"It's Fenton, isn't it?"

Lord Fenton looked up from his glass of sack and regarded Carey with a scowl.

"Do I know you?"

"Carey Fairfax." He held out his hand. "Seen you at White's, if I'm not mistaken. I think you must know Kedrington—my brother-in-law."

The name had a magic effect, as Carey had often noted. He did not hesitate to employ it to open doors, however, and this time it worked again.

"Of course, of course!" Fenton exclaimed affably. "Have a seat, Fairford."

"Fairfax, sir."

"Beg your pardon, I'm sure. What are you drinking? Kedrington here with you?"

"No, I'm alone. Just came to . . . er, visit an old army friend. Short trip and back to town in the morning."

"Pity. Why don't you stay a day or two, eh? I'd imagine you to be a sporting man, though the hunting's poor here, you know. Unless you like to fish? Good sport in that."

"I might be interested," Carey said.

He made himself more comfortable, thinking that he

might as well put in a word for himself, since Fenton had hinted that he might like company in whatever pursuit he had come to Sussex for. Fenton was well known as a sporting peer who did not hesitate to spread his blunt on the gaming tables in town and who appeared at every race meet and fisticuffs bout within a twenty-mile radius of London. His luck was said to be phenomenal, and he could pick a winner eight times out of ten.

Fenton, he learned during the course of the conversation, had newly acquired a rustic retreat in the county—a few acres with a small manor house—from which to organize parties of sea fishermen to go out in his yacht. It occurred to Carey that Lewes was some distance from the coast, but Fenton said his property was considerably nearer, just above Seaford, in fact, where he could keep his yacht.

After half an hour, Carey began to make his excuses, but Fenton ordered another round of ale, insisting that Carey be his guest, and the amiable conversation continued until sleep began to catch up with Carey. He found his head knocking against the table and raised it quickly.

"Beg pardon, Fenton. Long day, you know. Reckon I'd better take myself to bed."

"Dear boy, of course. Let me assist you upstairs."

Carey waved him off. "No, no, not to bother. Waiter'll help me."

"Get my direction from the landlord in the morning," Fenton called after Carey as he weaved unsteadily toward the door. "I'll be expecting you!"

Staring into the dregs of the coffeepot the following morning, Carey reflected that he should have confided in Fenton about Elena. He could use some help, and no doubt Fenton could supply it. It was too bad he had dropped off like that just when they were—

The last mists suddenly cleared from his head, and the truth darted in. Fenton had doctored his drink! It must have been that. Talking to the earl had just begun to revive him from his fatigue, and it was only after he'd had that second tankard of ale that he had suddenly—much too suddenly, he now realized—fallen asleep.

Damn and blast! He jumped up and hurriedly pulled on his clothes. Ten minutes later he had paid his shot and was riding in the direction the landlord had given him for Lord Fenton's manor.

He had no idea why Fenton should have slipped him some kind of drug, but it had to have something to do with Elena. Or Kedrington. Or both. He wished he'd paid more attention to his brother-in-law's comments about politics and such; he'd never cared much, because it didn't concern him directly, but he saw now that he'd been mistaken. Any sleeping snake was likely to rise up and sting you. Obviously, Fenton was up to no good, but Carey was feeling his way in the dark of his ignorance about the man.

Ten minutes out of Lewes, he pulled his horse up sharply as an idea occurred to him. If Fenton was up to something shady, he would naturally try to throw Carey off his trail. There was no point in continuing on to Fenton's place, then. He turned his mount in the direction of the house where his inquiries of the day before had led him to believe Elena was staying.

He reached the place half an hour later. It lay in the opposite direction from Fenton's manor, so if he had guessed wrong, he'd have lost precious time. He hoped he had not been wrong.

It was a cottage more than a house, with a gate and a low stone wall enclosing a flower garden between the wall and the front door, but its bucolic charm was lost on Carey as he stormed up to the door and knocked on it.

There was no answer, so he pounded harder. Shortly, a young woman carrying a milk bucket came around the side of the house and inquired what he thought he would accomplish making all that noise on a peaceful morning.

She was a pretty lass, with rosy cheeks and black ringlets, but Carey's former eye for the ladies was clouded today.

"Is Miss Melville in?"

"And who might be asking?"

"I'm her fiancé."

"Oh, yes? Then she has one more than she deserves, wicked girl. And I suppose you're some viscount's brother-in-law as well, are you?"

"What do you mean?"

"The young miss went off with some bloke calling himself her fee-*ahn*-ce not an hour ago. He also said he was this lord's brother."

Carey's irritation warred with his frustration, and he snapped, "I suppose this . . . this bloke called himself Carey Fairfax too?"

"Aye, that was the name."

"Was he a well-set-up chap, about forty, with brown hair and a scar above his lip?"

"That's him all right." The young woman eyed him doubtfully. "And who might you be?"

"Lord Fenton," Carey said promptly. "Did this Fairfax take Miss Melville away with him?"

"That he did."

"Did she go willingly?"

"That I couldn't say. She was willing enough to see him when he sent in word of who he was, but I didn't see them leave. I did see her in his carriage when they passed down the lane—there." She pointed toward the road running by the house.

"Is anyone else at home?" he asked.

"No, the lady's maid has gone out for bread, and the coachman's still out exercising the horses."

Carey thought furiously. Fenton had an hour's head start—but where would he have taken Elena? His house? Unlikely, for Carey knew where that was. His yacht! No, he knew where that was also—or approximately. Of course, Fenton could take Elena away in the boat and be out of range in little more than an hour.

"Is there some writing paper in the house?"

The girl shrugged and said she supposed there must be, then let him in by the garden door. He wrote a quick note, scanned it, then wrote another, identical to the first. He gave one note and some banknotes to the girl.

"Half of this is for you. Give the rest to the coachman when he comes back and tell him to send the letter from the nearest inn. He and the maid should wait here in case Miss Melville comes back. If I find her first, I'll send word what they're to do. What's your name?"

"Jenny, thank you, sir."

Carey planted a kiss on Jenny's cheek, and she jumped back with a startled but pleased "Oh!"

"Thank you too, Jenny."

Carey set off again, stopping only in Glynde for a fresh horse. The weather was uncomfortably warm, but as he neared the water, a light breeze sprang up. At last, rounding a slight rise of land before it sloped down again to a secluded little bay just east of the redbrick town of Seaford, he saw the tall mast of a large, seagoing yacht bobbing on the slight swell. He was in time!

Carey left his horse and slipped down to the water's edge on foot. Now that he was closer to the boat, which was still anchored not far from shore, he could see activity that looked like a crew making ready to sail. On the beach lay a dingy being loaded with supplies by a crewman. Carey looked around, but saw no one else on shore.

Then, as luck would have it, the man started up the beach toward the trees where Carey was hiding. Grinning, he waited for the man to stop and begin to unbutton his trousers. Then Carey stepped out and hit him over the head with the butt of his pistol. The man went down as silently as a stunned cow.

Carey rolled him over and pulled off the unbuttoned trousers, then the jacket and cap. Attired in this borrowed raiment, he made his way with a loping gait down to the dingy, climbed in, and rowed for the yacht.

He was undiscovered before he reached the yacht, anyone who might have seen him presumably believing him to be the crewman. His heart pounding, he climbed the ladder onto the boat and glanced quickly around. There was no one to be seen.

Walking lightly, he made a circuit of the boat, glancing into each window he passed. In the center cabin, he finally saw movement. He pressed his face against the glass and gasped.

"Elena!"

He pulled the door open, and Elena looked up from the cot she sat upon. Her face lit up when she saw him. "Carey!" she breathed. "I knew you would come."

"You did? I mean"—he glanced around—"are you alone? Are you all right? They haven't hurt you, have they?"

"No, no!" She rose and came to him, and he closed his arms around her. For a moment, there was only silence in the little cabin as they held each other tightly and silently reassured each other of their devotion.

Then Carey remembered their danger. "Is there no one else about?" he said.

"Only two crewmen. One went ashore for supplies. The other is below, I think. He must be asleep, for I have not heard him move about for some time. Indeed, I was thinking of jumping overboard. I can swim, you know, although I pretended I was afraid of the water, and—what are you doing in those clothes, Carey?"

"Disguise. Where's Fenton?"

"Is that who that man was? The men kept calling him 'my lord,' but he never said his name or what he wanted with me. He has gone to the village—I don't know its name, either, I'm afraid." She sighed and laid her head against his shoulder. "They wouldn't tell me where we were . . ."

"We must get out of here at once!" Carey said. "Before someone comes back. It's a stroke of luck that I got here while they were all out of the way, but our luck won't hold for long."

He stepped back, holding her by the shoulders, and

looked at her searchingly. "Will you come with me, dear?
Do you trust me? Do you . . . do you love me after all?"

"Oh, yes, Carey!" Elena's eyes filled with tears, but they
had no chance to spill over, for he kissed her swiftly, then
took her hand and led her out the door.

Quickly, they rounded the deck to where Carey had left
the dingy tied, still seeing no one. He helped Elena into the
little craft, then climbed in after her and rowed swiftly to
shore.

"My horse can carry us both," he said, "at least as far as
the next village."

Elena gasped as they passed the unconscious crewman,
still lying in the grove of trees where Carey had left him.

"He isn't dead, is he?"

To reassure her, he kneeled down and felt for the man's
pulse. It was still there, faint but steady.

"He'll be all right," he said, rising. "Wait a minute—I
want my own coat and pantaloons back. Turn around,
Elena."

She blushed, but obeyed, closing her eyes for good mea-
sure. She gave him a few minutes to dress, then opened her
eyes again.

And screamed.

Chapter 23

"I must say, Duncan," Lady Kedrington declared, "this is the smoothest ride I have had in any of our carriages. It is difficult to believe we are moving so swiftly!"

Lord Kedrington, far from showing appreciation for his wife's kind words about his new curricle—which he had done his valiant but futile best to prevent her from boarding that morning—said only that he was sure his horses were well aware of the pace they were setting.

"I wish you would put your bonnet back on, Antonia. You look a positive hoyden."

"Oh, pooh. Who is going to see us? And why should I not let my hair down in the company of my own husband? It feels wonderful to let the wind blow through it!"

"Perhaps you have forgotten that we are not on a pleasure drive."

Her face fell at that, and he instantly regretted having reminded her of their mission. He was not entirely sorry, after all, that she had come and told himself that when he found Elena, it would be better to have another woman along. That rationalization had also served to allay his own fear of the worst that could happen. He knew now that he had gained a reputation for being fearless in war because only his life had been at stake; when it came to Antonia's safety, he was far more cautious.

"I'm sorry, my love," he said. "I should not have said that."

"Yes, you should. I had forgotten. Oh, Duncan, do you

think we will find Carey in time? And what if we cannot find Elena? Would Lord Fenton really harm her?"

Kedrington thought he could, without a qualm, but did not say so. He had finally learned the identity of the man murdered in the East End—he had been an employee of Lord Fenton's who must have stumbled upon Fenton's involvement in the plot to steal the marbles. They would never know now.

"We'll find them," he assured her. "What is more likely is that Fenton was unaware of her presence in his vicinity after all, and she will be found perfectly safe at the house where Dimitri left her."

Unhappily, this proved not to be the case. They paused at Glynde to change horses and to wait for Dimitri, who had gone by a shorter route on horseback to the cottage, promising to report to them at Glynde if he found Elena safe.

They saw him pacing the yard of the only inn in the village when they pulled into it. Dimitri saw them and ran to take the horses' heads before the ostler could do so.

"She's not there!" he said. "I talked to a snippet of a milkmaid who said that two men had come by this morning asking about her. The first, who said his name was Carey Fairfax, took her away with him."

Antonia breathed a sigh of relief. "Then she must be on her way back with him to—"

The look on Dimitri's face stopped her. He handed up a piece of paper, which Kedrington took from her.

"The second man left this," Dimitri said.

Antonia read it over her husband's shoulder.

Duncan—

Fenton, giving my name, has taken Elena, probably to his yacht at Seaford. I am following.

C.F.

"The milkmaid said that your brother, Lady Kedrington,

was there less than an hour ago, and the ostler here says he stopped at this inn shortly after that."

"We must follow them, too!" Antonia declared. "We are not so far behind them now, Duncan."

"Nevertheless," the viscount said, handing the reins to the ostler, who had belatedly come out to see to their needs, "we must change horses here. Mine are spent, and even a poor pair will make good enough time on these roads. Antonia, go inside and rest for a few minutes. Dimitri will procure some refreshment for you."

Deciding that prompt obedience would get them on the road again faster than staying to argue the point, Antonia took Dimitri's hand to descend from the curricle. But when she reached the door of the inn, she turned and said, "Don't you leave without me!"

Kedrington grinned. "I would not dare!"

They were on their way again in twenty minutes. Dimitri rode alongside them now, Kedrington having absolutely forbidden him to ride ahead and confront Fenton on his own.

"You have not explained why Fenton should have taken Elena," Antonia said. "I understand that he is the mastermind behind the plot to steal the marbles, but what has Elena to do with it?"

Kedrington feathered a turn nicely, the job horses displaying a gratifying willingness to be guided by an expert hand. "I only suspected that he was the mastermind, although this action seems to confirm the circumstantial evidence. He probably hired Arthur Melville to organize the thing in order to keep his distance from it. Melville would have demanded a good deal of money to finance his various ambitions, but I doubt he had any feelings about the marbles one way or the other. My guess with regard to Elena is that Fenton simply snatched an unexpected opportunity when he learned somehow of Elena's presence in the neighborhood."

"An opportunity to do what?"

"Bargain. Perhaps he plans to hold her until he can leave

the country in this yacht of his. He may even plan to take her with him until he reaches France or wherever he is going."

Antonia shuddered. The mere possibility of never seeing Elena again might precipitate Carey into some rash action, never mind the possibility of harm coming to her.

At last they reached the shore and saw a ship lying at anchor a short distance away. Kedrington pulled his horses to a stop.

"Why are you stopping here? Let us go on—hurry!"

He smiled at her. "Didn't I say I would bring you to the seaside for a holiday? Let us make ourselves comfortable and consider the amusements available for our delight."

She had to laugh at that. "Don't be absurd. But what *are* you going to do?"

"We don't know what is happening down there. I'd best reconnoitre first. Dimitri will stay here with you."

Dimitri looked as if he would object to this plan, but Kedrington had disappeared into the sparse trees below them, as if by magic. Antonia watched him go, thinking, *So that is how he does it!* before smiling at Dimitri and shrugging her shoulders.

Kedrington thought he had heard a scream just before they stopped on the road, but he had not pointed that out to Antonia. It was not repeated, which was a hopeful sign, and now he could hear only low voices. He crept carefully toward them, pulling a pistol from inside his coat. He had not told Antonia he was armed. Although she doubtless expected it, he had judged it wiser not to mention the pistol—or the knife he had hidden in a leather sheath strapped to his leg.

As he came closer to the copse from which the voices came, Kedrington recognized Carey's, then saw him holding Elena close to him. Neither appeared harmed, although Carey was decidedly disheveled. On the ground near him lay a man's body.

And opposite them, his back to Kedrington, was Fenton.

He was speaking, and his habitual soft drawl had taken on a sinister overtone.

"Don't trouble yourself with thoughts of escape, Fairfax. It won't work, and in any case you wouldn't want to see your young lady harmed, would you? I assure you, I won't touch a hair on her head—if you cooperate."

"What do you want with us, Fenton?" Carey said.

"Only your company on a little sea voyage. We'll cross to the French coast, and there you'll be set free. I only need you to ensure my safe passage from England, you see."

"But you can just go now, alone. No one else has seen you, and by the time we can summon help, you will be long gone."

"Not long enough, dear boy. I always like to . . . er, adjust the odds in my favor when I can. That's why I'm such a successful gamester—one of the reasons. Being able to concentrate to the point of excluding even the noise of the dice being thrown is another."

While Fenton was thus singing his own praises, Kedrington slipped around behind him, then rose slightly from the concealment of the shrubbery. As he hoped, Carey spotted him but did not move a muscle except to press Elena's face to his chest so that she would not see him as well and inadvertently reveal his presence in some way.

"What was your purpose in all this, Fenton?" Carey asked, as Kedrington dropped out of sight again.

Fenton shrugged. "If you and your friends had only been so obliging as to report the stones missing, there might have been a delicious stink raised in the House."

"You did it for *entertainment*?" Carey sneered.

"Why not? But it was more than that. If I'd 'found' the missing marbles, I might have been a national hero. I do rather regret missing that, you know. As a last resort, I could have held them for ransom and turned a tidy profit."

"What about Melville? He might have given you away—even if he had not been apprehended."

Carey could see by the flicker of irritation in Fenton's

scowl that he was unaware of Melville's capture, but he only shrugged and said, "He was expendable."

"Were the Greeks he hired to steal the marbles expendable too? What did you tell them you were going to do with their stolen treasures?"

Fenton shrugged. "Who knows? I might have given them the real marbles and 'rescued' the fakes. A pity I never had the chance to work out all the permutations. It might have been most amusing to deceive absolutely everyone."

Carey grinned. "Pity you won't get away with it."

"Oh, but I will. I've been building quite a nice little nest egg for myself in France. I can live there, or somewhere else where no one will find me, quite comfortably for the rest of my life."

"You'll never get out of England, Fenton."

Fenton laughed. "My dear boy, I am as good as gone."

"I think not," Kedrington said then, standing upright and raising his pistol.

Fenton whirled around, but Kedrington was prepared and dropped to the ground again, so that Fenton's shot went well wide of the mark. Before he could fire again, Carey leapt forward and fell on top of him. Both men rolled down the slight slope Fenton had been standing on, and when they reached the bottom, Carey was on top. He dealt Fenton a single punishing blow to the jaw, and Fenton went limp.

Carey raised his fist again, looked disappointed when Fenton did not move, and lowered it.

"Nicely played," Kedrington said, coming up just then. "I am glad to see that high living has not slowed you down."

Carey got up, brushing the leaves from his clothes.

"I shouldn't bother, dear boy. Nothing short of burning it will improve that coat."

Carey laughed helplessly. "Duncan, you never change."

"I trust not."

"And I am once again grateful to you."

"Think nothing of it. Who's that over there?"

"Crewman. There's another on the boat somewhere."

Antonia burst into the copse at that moment, Dimitri directly behind her, and both stopped short when they saw who was still standing.

"Oh, thank goodness!" Antonia exclaimed, her hand to her heart. "We heard a shot."

"I think Fenton wounded that tree over there," Kedrington said. Antonia flung her arms around her husband's neck and covered his face with kisses.

"I'm so glad you're safe."

"So am I, my love, but you're embarrassing Dimitri."

"Tell him to look the other way."

But Dimitri was already embracing his sister. Carey, deprived of someone to hug, looked around him.

"I say, Duncan, what are we going to do with these fellows?"

The viscount, reminded of the late unpleasantness, looked down at Fenton, who was beginning to stir. A faint groan escaped him when Carey put his boot on his chest to keep him down.

"Perhaps you and Dimitri would be good enough to carry them up to my curricle—but for heaven's sake, lay something down on the seat before you put them on it. I won't have them ruining that new leather."

Carey grinned and saluted. "Yes, *sir!*"

"As for the other crewman . . ." Kedrington began, then looked toward the sea. The yacht was now some distance away, making for open sea. "Ah. It appears he has acquired a new boat and will not be joining our little party."

Kedrington looked down at Fenton, who was shaking his head as if to clear it. Suddenly, he reached down, took Fenton's chin in his hand, and demanded, "Where the devil does that key fit, Fenton? The puzzle has been exasperating me from the start."

A fleeting look of satisfaction crossed Fenton's face, but he said only, in a slurred voice that strove ineffectually for defiance, "What key?"

"You know what key."

Fenton sneered. "It belongs . . . to the house on . . . Cork

Street. Afterward . . . after it was lost . . . we just left the door opened. Nobody would have known the difference."

"Who killed the man who carried it?"

Fenton shrugged. "Not I. It was nothing to do with . . . with the man's work for me . . . sheer bad luck."

Kedrington looked disgusted, but he believed Fenton. He let him go abruptly, and Fenton slumped to the ground again. The two younger men lifted his limp body between them and made for the top of the rise, where Dimitri waited for Carey to have a hand free to retrieve the crewman, who was likewise showing signs of reviving and had been bound hand and foot.

Antonia, detaching herself from her husband's embrace, took Elena's hand and kissed her cheek.

"Are you all right, my dear?"

Elena smiled. "I am now, yes. Oh, dear Lady Kedrington, do you forgive me? I have caused you no end of trouble."

"Nonsense," Kedrington said briskly. "It was no fault of yours."

"Of course not," Antonia agreed. "But Elena—why did you not tell us about your true relationship with your brother?"

"I was afraid for him. And in the beginning, we were indeed estranged. Dimitri had become so . . . so obsessed with returning the Parthenon marbles to Greece that he had no thought in his mind for anything, or anyone, else. There was no reasoning with him. That was why I came to England in the first place—it was both an attempt to make him see reason and a cowardly reluctance on my part to see him destroy himself. When he followed me to London, however, I had to see him. I still loved him. I could not betray him, even when I really thought he was mixed up in the plot to steal the marbles."

"And you felt you had to make a choice between your brother and Carey."

Elena nodded, unable to say more. Antonia dug a handkerchief out of her pocket and dabbed at Elena's eyes with it, whispering soothing things to her until she finally gave a watery smile and thanked her.

"And you, too, my lord—that is, Duncan."

"It was my pleasure to assist in any way I could," he replied with a bow. "Besides, the sooner Carey moves out of my house, the sooner I can resume my peaceful retirement. I warn you, Elena, he is like an undisciplined puppy when kept indoors."

Smiling, she said, "I shall train him before he knows it, you'll see."

"Well, then, you had better go and begin at once."

Elena gave Antonia's hand a last squeeze and went to join her brother and her lover. Lord and Lady Kedrington lingered behind a little longer.

"Now that you are all safe," Antonia said, with a little sigh, "I must confess that I have not enjoyed myself so much since the day I got tipsy on champagne and you proposed to me."

He raised her hand to kiss it. "That was not precisely why I proposed to you."

"Perhaps not, but you know to a nicety when to make a strategic move—as you demonstrated here today."

"That was not strategy, only brute force. There was no time for subtleties."

"Nonetheless, I wish you would teach me—"

"Certainly not."

"How did you know what I was going to say?"

"It doesn't matter. I shall teach you nothing, my dear Lady Mischief, that would even remotely prompt you to become embroiled in such an escapade again."

"I don't see how I could have helped it—this time."

He looked toward heaven as if seeking wisdom from a greater power.

"Anyway," Antonia said, "I shall have to stay out of mischief a little while."

"And what miracle will keep you from it?"

She smiled. "A miracle indeed. You did not let me tell you my second story the other night, Duncan."

He frowned for a moment. "Oh, yes—you did say you had two stories. What was it?"

"I shall tell you only the happy ending."

He stopped and faced her, laughing. "Well, what is it? You are the most exasperating woman!"

She looked up at him, then lowered her eyes as a flush came over her face. In a low voice she told him, "I have suspected it for some weeks, but was not certain until just the other day, but . . . you are finally going to be a father, my dear."

He made no move and was silent for so long that she finally raised her eyes to his. There was a glow in them that she had never seen before, and it was even warmer than the light she had seen there when she first told him she loved him.

"Oh, my love . . ."

It was a long time before they joined the others, but they all waited patiently.